"It was no mis~~take~~, Jessica," Dane ~~argued~~

"You wanted me as much as I wanted you."

"I don't deny that—" she bit out the words "—but it was lust, nothing more, and I'm ashamed."

He released her so unexpectedly that she staggered, his height and breadth menacing in the darkness as he demanded harshly. "Do you mean that?"

There was a certain urgency about Dane at that moment that her tortured brain couldn't grasp, and she pushed trembling hands through her hair as she leaned against the door frame for support.

"Yes," she said at last in a tired husky voice. "Yes, I mean it."

A prolonged tense silence followed before he spoke again. "In that case, Jessica, you need have no fear that I'll touch you again." With pain-filled eyes she watched him walk away.

YVONNE WHITTAL

dance of the snake

Harlequin Books

TORONTO • NEW YORK • LOS ANGELES • LONDON
AMSTERDAM • PARIS • SYDNEY • HAMBURG
STOCKHOLM • ATHENS • TOKYO • MILAN

Harlequin Presents first edition November 1982
ISBN 0-373-10550-9

Original hardcover edition published in 1981
by Mills & Boon Limited

CHAPTER ONE

JESSICA NEAL faced her father across the wide expanse of his polished desk and saw the incredulity mirrored in his dark brown eyes as he lowered himself into his swivel chair. The leather creaked beneath his weight, jarring her taut nerves, but the set of her small, rounded chin lost none of its determination. She had applied for a post in Louisville, she had signed the contract which would bind her for a year as an assistant to Dr O'Brien and his partner, and there was nothing anyone could do to alter the situation. This was the information with which she had confronted her father, a retired medical man himself, and this was what he seemed to be finding so difficult to accept.

'What about your decision to specialise in paediatrics?' Jonathan Neal demanded, and Jessica flinched inwardly.

'That was your decision, Daddy, not mine.'

Her voice, the attractive huskiness pronounced in moments of stress, hovered in the air between them accusingly. She had not intended to accuse, for no one knew better than she did how her father had had to smother his disappointment when Gregory, four years her senior, had announced that he intended becoming an engineer instead of a doctor like their father. It had taken a considerable effort to come to terms with his son's decision, but Jonathan Neal had succeeded, and his happiness had known no bounds when Jessica had finally announced her decision to follow in her father's footsteps.

Looking at him now, Jessica felt a pang of regret. She had spoken without thinking, and she cursed herself for not having phrased her statement with more care. He raised a weary hand and pushed it through springy grey hair, and the eyes that met hers barely concealed the anxiety in their depths.

'Have I pushed you too hard, Jessica?'

She was being given the opportunity to rectify her rash statement, and on this occasion she replied with infinite gentleness and care. 'I've always appreciated your help and your guidance, Daddy.'

'But you think it's time you went your own way?' he filled in what Jessica had been so loath to add.

'I must pave my own way in life, and do what I think best.'

Silence descended on her father's study; an explosive silence filled with frustration and anger as Jonathan Neal rose from his chair and trailed his hand absently along the thick medical volumes in the shelves against the wall behind his desk. He was unaware of what he was doing, Jessica knew this, and the explosion, when it came, was no surprise to her.

'Dammit, Jessica! Someone with your level of intelligence shouldn't be allowed to stagnate in some godforsaken place like Louisville!'

His voice was harsh, his manner aggressive, but on this occasion Jessica stood firm instead of relenting as she had done so often in the past.

'I doubt if I shall be stagnating in Louisville, Daddy. I shall be treating all kinds of people for various kinds of ailments, and in doing so I shall at last discover what it's like to be a real doctor.'

'But that's something you could do right here at the General.'

'No!' Anger darkened her heavily-lashed eyes until they were the exact colour of her father's. 'I've done nothing during these past two years but administer to the patients whose ailments senior doctors considered too trivial to be bothered with.'

'That's a libellous statement!'

'It happens to be the truth!' They glared at each other for a few brief seconds, then Jessica's small, slim body relaxed visibly, but the hint of cynicism continued to hover about her generous mouth. 'Everyone is so busy qualifying themselves in the various fields of medicine, or waving the banner of their seniority about, that I think they've forgotten the essence of doctoring.'

'And you imagine you'll find things different in Louisville?' Jonathan challenged.

'I have every reason to believe I shall.'

A lengthy silence prevailed, then Jonathan Neal's chair creaked protestingly once more beneath his weight when he sat down and rested his elbows on the desk.

'It would be pointless for me to say I'm not disappointed.'

'And Mother will naturally be horrified,' Jessica nodded.

Her father had a weary look about him now as he glanced up at her. 'Do you want me to break the news to her?'

Jessica shook her head and stepped around the desk to plant an impulsive kiss on her father's lined cheek. 'I'll tell her this evening after dinner.'

Alone in her room some minutes later Jessica realised that a great deal of her tension had deserted her. The worst hurdle had been crossed successfully, and all that remained now was for her to enlighten her mother, but Amelia Neal was not as formidable a hurdle as her husband.

Jessica bathed and changed for dinner, exchanging the smell of disinfectant for that of cologne before she stepped back a little to examine herself in the full-length mirror against the wall. Her appraisal of herself was brief and without the usual interest women had in their outward appearance. She had never bothered much about what she was wearing. It was more important to feel comfortable and look neat, while her dark brown hair, curling softly about the fine bone structure of her face, was kept short to allow her the maximum control with the minimum of fuss.

She turned away from the mirror, unconcerned, but had she lingered to observe herself more critically she might have noticed the dark, finely arched brows above equally dark eyes, and the enviably smooth, creamy complexion of her healthy skin stretching across slightly raised cheekbones down to a firm, rounded chin. The nose was small and neatly chiselled above the full, faintly sensuous mouth, and her small, slender figure with its gentle, feminine curves had caused many a male student to feel protective towards her, rather than passionate. This had not troubled her during her stint at varsity, and neither did it trouble her now as a fully fledged doctor. There had been no time to indulge in lighthearted affairs. She had been one of a half-dozen girls among a bevy of male medical students, and most of her time and energy had been spent on proving herself capable of producing similar, if not better results than her male counterparts. As a newly qualified doctor the same had applied, and even now, after two years, she still felt that urgent need to prove herself.

It was not of herself that Jessica was thinking when she went downstairs that evening to join her parents for dinner. She was thinking of her mother, and how she would react to the news that her daughter would soon be leaving home.

Dinner was over too swiftly that evening for Jessica's liking, but when her father tactfully retired to his study, leaving Jessica alone in the living-room with her mother, she knew that the awful moment had come.

There was no point in delaying, and Jessica voiced her plans quickly and simply as she sat facing the small, attractively rounded figure of her mother in the chair opposite her own. Amelia Neal took it all surprisingly well, and without interrupting, until Jessica's voice drifted off into silence.

'Does your father know?' was all Amelia was concerned with at that precise moment and, when Jessica nodded, a strange expression flitted across her sensitive features. It was a mixture of anxiety, regret and relief, and long after Jessica had gone to bed that evening she still wondered at what had exactly gone through her mother's mind at that moment.

The time for Jessica's departure from Johannesburg drew near with a swiftness that left no room for regret, but Jonathan and Amelia avoided the subject as if it were the plague, forcing Jessica to do the same. It was on the eve of her departure, after they had sat through a silent, uncomfortable meal, that Jonathan Neal once again voiced his disapproval loudly, and to the accompaniment of a clenched fist crashing down on to the table that made Jessica and her mother jump.

'I think you're a fool to wave aside the opportunities which a city like Johannesburg could offer you. If it's a private practice you wanted, then I could have set you up on your own, but to go and bury yourself in the remoteness of the northern Transvaal is the most ridiculous thing I've ever heard of.' The delicate glassware and china rattled protestingly once more when his fist descended on to the table for the second time. 'I'm damned if I understand it!'

Jessica met her mother's anxious glance across the table, and smiled at her reassuringly before she replied to her father's outburst.

'You've always been too ambitious on my behalf, Daddy, and I've always appreciated it, but before I tie myself down to further study, or a practice of my own, I must reach some sort of stability in my profession. I've

been a qualified medical doctor for two years now, but as
yet I haven't been given the opportunity to make full use
of my knowledge, and this is what I believe I shall be
given the chance to do in Louisville.'

Jonathan Neal seemed to sag in his chair at the head of
the table. 'Did you have to sign a contract for a year?'

Jessica met his glance steadily. 'That was the required
period, and I'm happy with it.'

'What about marriage, Jessica?' Amelia Neal's query
interrupted the tense silence, and Jessica's expression went
curiously blank as she diverted her attention to the woman
seated opposite her.

'Marriage, Mother?'

'Yes, *marriage*,' Amelia stressed the word. 'For years
now I've sat back and listened to you and your father
discuss your professional career in detail as a doctor, but
lately I've come to the conclusion that, in the process,
you've forgotten how to be a woman.' Her hazel eyes
were suddenly filled with deep concern. 'Don't you want
a husband and children, Jessica?'

Taken aback, Jessica said weakly, 'Of course I would
like to marry some day and have children, but——'

'Then may I suggest that you start thinking seriously
about it. You're almost twenty-eight, and you're not getting any younger, you know.'

'For goodness' sake, Amelia, there's plenty of time!'

'No, there isn't, Jonathan,' her mother contradicted her
father, but her glance was almost apologetic. 'Don't think
I haven't been aware of your disappointment at Gregory's
decision to study engineering instead of medicine, and
don't think that I'm not aware of how you have pinned
all your hopes and desires on Jessica since the day she
announced that she wanted to study medicine, but you've
forgotten one very important factor, my dear. Jessica is a
woman.'

'I should hope I'm a woman,' Jessica laughed to

alleviate the tension.

'Then what about finding yourself a nice, comfortable husband, and presenting us with a few healthy grand-children?' her mother charged.

'Gregory's wife will soon be presenting you with your first grandchild.'

'I'm not talking about Gregory,' Amelia gestured impatiently. 'I'm talking about you.'

Amusement lurked in Jessica's eyes as she glanced at her father briefly before replying. 'I can't promise anything until I've found the right man.'

'And how will you do that when you look at them all as if they were specimens on the examination slab?' Amelia demanded indignantly.

'I think,' Jessica began after a thoughtful silence, 'when the right man comes along the examination slab will be the farthest thing from my mind.'

'I hope you're right about that,' Amelia remarked fervently.

Jessica exchanged glances with her father and, for the first time in days, she saw that gleam of devilment lurking in his eyes as he leaned towards her mother and clasped her hand across the table.

'Did I ever look at you as if you were a specimen on a slab?' he wanted to know.

'No, dear,' Amelia replied at once, 'but then I made very sure that you saw me as a woman in an unprofessional way.'

'Mother!' Jessica exclaimed in mock horror. 'Are you saying that——'

'I'm not saying anything of the kind,' Amelia interrupted, her cheeks going a delicate pink. 'And don't change the subject.'

'What your mother meant was that anatomy had nothing to do with what we saw in each other,' Jonathan explained, tongue in cheek. 'Isn't that so, my dear?'

Amelia Neal observed her husband and daughter for a moment in speechless silence, then she said resignedly, 'Why do I have the feeling that you're both having fun at my expense?'

'We couldn't resist it, could we, Daddy?' Jessica laughed mischievously. 'For a woman of your age you still blush so beautifully.'

'Don't be absurd! I was trying to——'

'I know, Mother,' Jessica interrupted, sobering at once when she glimpsed the concern in her mother's glance. 'Falling in love is more than just physical. It's a union of the mind and heart as well, and that's how I'll know when I've met the right man. There will have to be a mental as well as a physical attraction and, until I find someone who qualifies in that respect, I prefer to remain unattached.'

The trend of the conversation had suddenly altered from the lighthearted to the serious and, for the first time since learning of Jessica's plans, Amelia asked, 'Where will you be staying?'

'Dr O'Brien very kindly offered me the use of a small cottage within the grounds of his home. It's fully furnished, I believe, and I shall have a private telephone at my disposal.'

'I hope you've made the right decision, Jessica.'

Jonathan Neal's remark did not require an answer, neither did he wait for one as he pushed back his chair and rose from the table. Jessica and her mother followed suit, and the rest of the evening was spent packing the items Jessica intended sending by train on to Louisville.

It was a freezingly cold morning in July as Jessica drove northwards to Louisville. The frost had lain white and crisp on the lawns surrounding her parents' home, and she was some distance from Johannesburg before her Alfa's heater vent had any effect on her chilled feet and hands. She had a long journey ahead of her and, at a rough guess, she would not reach her destination until mid-afternoon, but it was of some consolation to know that she was heading towards a warmer climate.

How warm it would be Jessica only discovered when she crossed the Soutpansberg mountain range that afternoon, and it was when the road dropped down into bushveld country that she realised she was now in the land of the baobab trees where she had heard that the winters were warm, and the summers blisteringly hot. She had been aware of the change in the climate for some time now, and she had long since exchanged her fleece-lined jacket, slacks and thick sweater for a cool blouse and cotton skirt. She glanced about her with interest, and it was then that she glimpsed Louisville nestling close to the foot of the mountains.

Jessica stopped at the filling station to refuel the Alfa, and while the attendant did what was necessary, she wandered across to the office to ask for directions to Dr O'Brien's home.

'You'll have to go back a little,' the young woman behind the desk informed her, pointing the way Jessica had come. 'Turn left at the old stone church, then right two blocks farther. You can't miss Dr O'Brien's house. It's on a corner, and it's the only two-storied house in that street.'

Jessica thanked her and, aware of the girl's curious glance following her, she walked out of the building towards her car. She paid the attendant the required amount and drove away quickly.

Five minutes later Jessica was easing herself out of her car once more, and walking rather stiffly up the path towards the modern two-storied house with its large windows and beautifully terraced garden. The front door, with panelled glass windows on either side of it, stood open, giving Jessica a glimpse of the spacious entrance hall where expensive rugs lay scattered casually on the polished floor. Jessica thumbed the button beside the door, and a bell chimed somewhere in the silent house.

'If that's you, Dr Neal, then please come straight in. I'll be with you in a minute,' a woman's voice instructed almost at once, and Jessica stepped curiously into the cool interior, her glance travelling in the direction from which the voice had come. A woman appeared in the doorway to Jessica's right. She was tall and beautifully proportioned, and she stopped abruptly at the sight of Jessica, a mixture of humour and uncertainty flashing across her perfectly chiselled face. 'Oh, I'm dreadfully sorry. I was expecting Dr Neal to arrive, and I naturally presumed——'

'I *am* Dr Neal,' Jessica interrupted.

'*You're* Dr Neal?' Dark eyes widened in surprise, and she stared at Jessica speechlessly for a second or two, then, for some curious reason, she burst out laughing, and it was some time before she finally managed to control herself. 'You must forgive me, my dear,' she apologised weakly, brushing the moisture from her eyes with the tips of her fingers. 'I just couldn't help myself.'

Jessica's back was rigid as she stared up at this tall woman with her dark hair combed back from her face and coiled into a chignon in the nape of her neck. 'You find it amusing that I'm a woman?'

'Yes—no—oh, heavens, this is getting worse. Come and sit down while I try to explain.' She led the way into the large living-room with its attractive mixture of modern and antique furnishings, and gestured Jessica into a chair before seating herself elegantly in the chair opposite. 'My husband has talked of nothing else these past weeks but of the new *man* he was expecting,' she explained, merriment sparkling in her eyes, 'and I'm just dying to see his face when he discovers that you're a woman.'

Taken aback, Jessica stared at the woman facing her.

She had never once given it a thought that they might be expecting a man, and the discovery disturbed her considerably. 'Dr O'Brien never queried whether I was male or female, and as our correspondence progressed I naturally presumed that he knew I was a woman.'

'Well, he's certainly going to be surprised when he finds out.' The woman's eyes, a shade darker than Jessica's, crinkled at the corners with apologetic humour. 'Forgive me, my dear, but I'm Vivien O'Brien, as you must have guessed, and now that I've met you I'm extremely curious to know what the "J" stands for.'

'Jessica.'

'Shylock's daughter,' Vivien O'Brien remarked absently.

'I beg your pardon?'

'*The Merchant of Venice.*'

'Oh, yes,' Jessica smiled faintly, her brow clearing. 'My mother was an avid reader of Shakespeare's plays.'

Vivien O'Brien was somewhere in her mid-thirties, Jessica guessed, and her figure still possessed a slender elegance which was as enviable as her height.

'You must think me extremely rude,' Vivien interrupted Jessica's observation. 'Could I offer you something to drink? A cup of tea, perhaps?'

'I would prefer to get myself settled, if you don't mind,' Jessica replied politely. 'It's been a long journey, and I'm rather tired.'

'Yes, of course. I'll show you——' The shrill ring of the telephone in the hall interrupted her. 'Excuse me a moment.'

Vivien crossed the room and stepped into the hall, but from the expression on her face when she glanced towards Jessica a few moments later, the caller could have been no one else but her husband.

'Yes, Peter, Dr Neal has arrived,' Vivien assured him, her eyes dancing with merriment as they met Jessica's. 'I was on the point of taking ... er ... Dr Neal across to the cottage. If you're on your way home, then you should find us there.' There was a brief pause, then Vivien said gaily, 'See you soon, darling.'

'That was Dr O'Brien?' Jessica queried, rising from her chair as Vivien re-entered the living-room.

'Yes,' Vivien nodded, obviously finding it difficult to hide her inner amusement. 'He will be home in a few minutes, but in the meantime I'll show you the way to the cottage.' Jessica followed her out into the garden where the rays of the late afternoon sun seemed to bathe everything in gold. 'If you take your car round the corner you'll find the entrance to the cottage, and there's a carport at your disposal.'

'Thank you.'

Vivien obviously took a short cut through the garden, for when Jessica drove through the private entrance to the thatched cottage she found her waiting there with a small bunch of keys dangling from her fingers.

The cottage was not as small as Jessica had imagined it would be. There were two bedrooms, a dining-room, lounge, kitchen and bathroom, and all the rooms were spacious and airy.

'This was originally my husband's consulting-rooms until we altered it some years ago into a guest cottage. When Peter started thinking of taking on an assistant we thought the cottage would be absolutely ideal for that purpose,' Vivien explained while taking Jessica on a tour of her new home. 'It looks rather bare, I'm afraid, but it leaves you plenty of room to add your own personal touches to the inside appearance.'

Jessica allowed her glance to travel over the neat pine-wood furniture with its bright floral coverings in the lounge, and felt instantly at home. 'I'm certain I shall find it very comfortable.'

Vivien's warm smile deepened with pleasure. 'There's

a private telephone at your disposal. We've also installed an air-conditioner to make the summer months tolerable, and, knowing how busy you're going to be, you will have your evening meal with Peter and myself.'

'That's very kind of you, but I would prefer to manage on my own as much as possible,' Jessica declined politely, but firmly.

'Very well, I accept that, but only on one condition,' Vivien conceded. 'You will eat with us this evening, and if, in future, you're kept out late on some or other case, I hope you'll allow me to make arrangements for a meal to be left in your oven for you.'

'Thank you, I would appreciate that,' Jessica found herself relenting.

'That's settled, then, and——' Vivien broke off abruptly at the sound of footsteps coming along the path outside the cottage. 'That will be Peter.'

'Are you there, Vivien?' a pleasant male voice demanded.

'Yes, darling.' Vivien paused to wink mischievously at Jessica. 'Do come in. We're in the lounge.'

Tall, lean and fair, Peter O'Brien stepped into the cottage and, like Vivien, he halted abruptly at the sight of the small, slim young woman standing beside his wife.

'Good afternoon,' he nodded briefly, his blue eyes casting a searching glance about the room before focussing on Jessica once more. 'I'm afraid I was under the impression that Dr Neal was unmarried.'

'Please allow me to introduce you, Peter,' Vivien intervened smoothly. 'This is Dr Jessica Neal. Dr Neal, I'd like you to meet my husband, Peter O'Brien.'

Jessica's own sense of humour was beginning to stir at the look of shocked surprise on Dr O'Brien's lean face, but she could not entirely discard her wariness as she said politely, 'How do you do, Dr O'Brien.'

'Well, I . . . Good gracious, I had no idea . . . I never

once thought that . . .'

Vivien's laughter rang out clearly at the sight of her husband shaking his fair head in helpless confusion. 'I've never yet known you to stumble in your efforts to find the right words, darling.'

'Quite frankly, I'm stunned,' Peter O'Brien confessed.

Jessica met his blue gaze directly, her prickly pride severely suppressed. 'Does my being a woman make a difference?'

'Certainly not!' the words almost exploded from the man before her. 'Your qualifications are excellent, Dr Neal, and that's all I'm concerned with. If I appear taken aback because you're a woman, then it's merely because I took it for granted that you were a man, and I never thought to query it.' He held out his hand and Jessica found hers taken in a warm clasp. 'Welcome to Louisville, Dr Neal, and may your stay here with us be a happy one.'

'Thank you, Dr O'Brien,' Jessica smiled with an inward sigh of relief.

'Well, I think we should give Jessica the opportunity to settle in, and freshen up,' Vivien intervened, her warm glance questioning as it rested on Jessica. 'You don't mind if I call you Jessica, do you?'

'I don't mind at all,' Jessica replied a little breathlessly.

'Dinner is at seven, my dear,' Vivien told her brightly. 'If you take the flagstone path you'll find it a short cut through the garden to our home.'

'Thank you.'

'We'll see you later, then,' Vivien smiled, linking her arm through her husband's, but at the door she paused once more to glance back at Jessica. 'Don't dress specially for the occasion. Dinner in our home is nearly always casual.'

For some time after they had left Jessica remained where she was, drinking in the silence and the utter peace of her surroundings. She was going to like it here, she knew that now, and an inner excitement provided her with the energy to want to offload her car as quickly as possible.

A large black woman came bustling along the path towards Jessica as she emerged from the cottage, and two rows of white, shining teeth were bared in a friendly smile. Her name was Lettie, she introduced herself, and Mrs O'Brien had instructed her to help the young Missy Doctor carry her things into the cottage.

To have refused her help would have meant offending her, and a half hour later Jessica was decidedly glad that she had allowed Lettie to help her carry her belongings into her new home, for her limbs were stiff and aching, and it gave her plenty of time afterwards to soak in a relaxing bath.

She would unpack later, Jessica decided, opening one of her suitcases and selecting a cool, wrinkle-free dress which looked neat but casual when she finally glanced at herself in the mirror, and after slipping her feet into a pair of high-heeled sandals, which added at least a few inches to her height, she was almost ready to face Dr O'Brien and his wife for dinner.

An hour later Jessica was seated once again in Vivien O'Brien's spacious and beautifully furnished living-room, and on this occasion her appearance did not cause the disturbance it had done earlier.

'Wine, Jessica?' Dr O'Brien offered.

'That would be nice, thank you, Dr O'Brien.'

'Peter,' he corrected, filling a long-stemmed glass with crimson liquid and handing it to her. 'If we're going to work well together, then I would prefer to drop the formalities as from this moment.'

Jessica smiled her agreement and sipped at her wine before remarking enquiringly, 'You mentioned in your correspondence that you have a partner.'

'Yes,' he nodded, lowering his long, lean body into a chair, and stretching out his legs before him. 'His name is Dane Trafford.'

'Dane is a bachelor,' Vivien explained in more detail, 'and he's a little bit of a rake as far as the townspeople are concerned.'

'That's enough, Vivien,' Peter O'Brien scowled disapprovingly.

'It's only right that Jessica should know what kind of man she's going to be closely associated with,' Vivien argued calmly.

'Dane is a fine doctor,' her husband protested.

'I've never questioned that,' Vivien replied as Jessica sat back to observe this verbal altercation between husband and wife. 'The problem is that Dane's personal life has certainly given the people of Louisville much to talk and speculate about.'

'His personal life is none of our business.'

'Peter, you know I'm very fond of Dane, and, even though he's a bit of a rake at times, he has such likeable ways when he decides to put aside his cynicism.'

Peter O'Brien sipped at his wine and shrugged carelessly. 'He most likely has his reasons for being cynical about certain things.'

'I don't question that either,' Vivien acknowledged, 'but you can't expect the people not to talk among themselves when that Summers woman arrives from Pretoria every so often to move in with him for the weekend.'

'Sylvia Summers is a beautiful woman,' Peter remarked, mischief dancing in his blue eyes.

'Oh, yes, I suppose so,' Vivien snorted. 'If you approve of the type of woman who wears the minimum of clothes in order to leave nothing to the imagination, then one could say that she's beautiful.'

'Jealous, Vivien?'

Vivien O'Brien flashed her husband a smile that was

devoid of malice, but filled with obvious humour. 'Darling, if I didn't know that you loved me to distraction then I might have been.' Peter's bark of laughter sobered her once more. 'As I was saying, his affair with Sylvia Summers has certainly not endeared him to the simple country folk living here, and he has only himself to blame for that.'

'Don't put Jessica off Dane before she's even met him,' Peter warned humorously, and Vivien's dark glance slid across to where Jessica sat so quietly.

'Jessica, my dear, despite all I've said, Dane has an undeniable charm which would make any woman feel that she was something special. The women frown upon his behaviour, but they nevertheless crowd out the waiting-room to see him specifically.' She smiled suddenly and added warningly, 'Take care, my dear.'

'Of Dr Trafford, or his lady friend?' Jessica asked carefully.

'Of both,' Vivien replied, her glance becoming speculative. 'The Summers woman may not do more than scratch your eyes out, but Dane might tear your heart out, and it's the latter I'm afraid of.'

'I'm a doctor, Vivien,' Jessica reminded her, 'and I have been closely involved with all kinds of men ever since my days as a student.'

'You're also a woman, don't forget that, and a very attractive and feminine woman too, if I may say so.'

'You should get together with my mother,' Jessica laughed with a touch of embarrassment. 'She has, during the past years, considered me anything but feminine.'

'That's because, like most mothers, she wanted a daughter with a tendency towards frills and lace, but instead you wandered into the world of men, and she most probably considers that somewhere along the way you have forgotten how to be a woman.' Vivien's remarkable insight very nearly succeeded in taking Jessica's breath away. 'I'm right, aren't I?' Vivien demanded.

'You're absolutely right,' Jessica admitted, unable to hide her surprise.

Peter O'Brien cleared his throat and set aside his empty glass. 'Forgive me for interrupting, but my insides are beginning to cry out for sustenance.'

'How like a man!' Vivien teased. 'They can think of nothing else but food.'

Over dinner Peter discussed with Jessica the routine he and Dr Trafford followed, but she knew it would be largely a case of helping out where she would be needed and, later that evening, when she returned to her cottage, she found that she had plenty to think about. The O'Briens were a pleasant, likeable couple, but Dr Dane Trafford was an unknown quantity. Vivien's remarks had stirred the surface of her interest, but she had no intention of spending the rest of the night wondering about Peter O'Brien's partner, and the woman who so openly lived with him at times as his mistress.

Jessica telephoned her parents instead to inform them of her safe arrival, and, after unpacking a few things, she made herself a cup of coffee and went to bed. She had the entire weekend ahead of her to settle into the cottage. She would have to stock up the cupboards in the kitchen, and she was going to enjoy these few days of relaxation before plunging in at the deep end on the Monday morning as Peter O'Brien had promised.

CHAPTER TWO

THE weekend passed much too swiftly for Jessica, who was beginning to relish the thought of making a home for herself in the neat, whitewashed cottage that nestled at the far end of the O'Briens' colourful garden. Here she could be a woman as well as a doctor, and that ought to please her mother, she thought with a wry smile.

Peter O'Brien's consulting-rooms were in an old house just off the town's main street, a house which had been altered to suit the purpose, and when Jessica entered the building on that Monday morning with Peter, the first person she met was Sister Emily Hansen. Elderly and professional, Sister Hansen overcame her initial shock at discovering that the new doctor was a woman, and welcomed Jessica into the fold with something that bordered on motherly warmth.

'Dr Trafford telephoned a few minutes ago,' Sister Hansen informed Peter eventually. 'He was called out to the Grayson farm early this morning, and he'll be in a little later than usual this morning.'

'Damn!' Peter muttered under his breath. 'What's the problem?'

'One of the labourers was apparently gored by an angry bull, and Dr Trafford is bringing him in to the hospital for possible surgery,' Sister Hansen explained.

Peter frowned and glanced down at Jessica. 'This means you'll be on your own for a while. Do you think you'll manage?'

'Yes, of course,' Jessica replied calmly and with a confidence she had inherited from her father.

'Good girl,' Peter smiled down at her. 'If there's anything you want to know, then you have only to ask Sister Hansen, and I'll be at the hospital if I'm needed urgently.'

Moments later, when his Mercedes disappeared down the street, Sister Hansen stepped out from behind her desk in the corner of the waiting-room, and gestured Jessica to follow her.

'These two rooms are Dr O'Brien's,' she indicated as they went down the passage. 'These two are Dr Trafford's, and these here will be yours, Dr Neal.'

'Why two rooms?' Jessica asked curiously, entering the larger of the two and glancing about her as she lifted her medical bag on to the desk.

'When the waiting-room is crowded, two rooms are a blessing,' Sister Hansen explained briskly. 'It enables you to see to two patients almost simultaneously.'

From the hook behind the door Sister Hansen removed a short white coat, but her expression was comically rueful as she glanced from it to Jessica. It was obvious, even from a distance, that the size was several times too large for Jessica, and she laughed a little selfconsciously.

'It doesn't matter,' Jessica set her mind at rest and, opening her bag, brought out a neatly folded white jacket which she shook out and draped across the chair behind the desk. 'I brought along my own,' she explained to the relieved Sister Hansen. 'I've never yet found a size to fit, so I had a few jackets specially made for me.'

'That was very sensible of you,' Emily Hansen smiled, taking in Jessica's smallness, but she tactfully said no more.

'At what time do you expect the first patient to arrive?' Jessica asked, glancing at her wrist watch.

'Any moment now.' The Sister tilted her head in a listening attitude. 'If I'm not mistaken, then I hear someone in the waiting-room at this very moment.'

'Then I suppose you'd better send whoever it is in.'

With an outward calmness that belied a sudden spurt of ridiculous nervousness, Jessica's steady, questioning glance met Sister Hansen's. 'There's no reason to wait, is there?'

'None at all, Dr Neal.'

The door closed behind Sister Hansen's sturdy figure and, with a few seconds at her disposal, Jessica slipped on her white jacket over her cool cotton frock, and familiarised herself with the small clinical room in an effort to steady herself. The room was not overcrowded, but it contained everything that she might possibly need. A high bunk, neatly covered with waterproofing and a sheet, stood behind a screen for examination purposes, and a glass cabinet, which contained the necessary sterilised instruments and drugs, stood in the opposite corner beside the door leading into the adjoining room.

After walking the spacious wards of a city hospital, this was something new and strange to Jessica, but the feeling of strangeness wore off soon after the first patient was shown in.

As the morning progressed Jessica could not avoid being aware of the various reactions from the patients when they discovered that she was a woman. There was surprise, then uncertainty, and finally a wary submission to her ministrations, but she had the feeling that they were no longer in doubt by the time they walked out clutching a prescription in their hands.

Jessica's most difficult patient that morning was a large, portly, sunburnt farmer who gaped at her in dismay and uncertainty as he clutched at his wide-brimmed, sweaty hat.

'Has Dr O'Brien taken on another nurse as well as a new doctor?' he demanded in a gravelly, heavily accented voice, and Jessica glanced quickly at the name on the file before answering.

'I'm not a nurse, Mr Boshoff, I'm a doctor.'

Eyes of an indiscriminate colour widened in disbelief. 'You're the new doctor?'

'That's right.' Jessica's glance was cool and professional. 'What ails you, Mr Boshoff?'

'Well, I have this cough, you see, Doctor, and it hurts right here,' he explained at last, stabbing at a spot on his vast, khaki-clad chest with a thick forefinger. 'I was wondering if you couldn't give me something for it,' he added, eyeing her dubiously.

Jessica rose from behind her desk. 'I shall have to examine you first.'

'Examine me?'

The man backed away from her, and she was reminded of a startled horse rearing on to its hind legs, but she deliberately paid no attention for fear of laughing as she pointed to the stool beside the examination bunk. 'Take off your shirt, Mr Boshoff, and sit down over there.'

'I'm not taking my shirt off in front of a woman!' the man thundered indignantly, clutching his hat against him like a shield. 'Just give me something for my cough, then I won't trouble you further.'

Jessica sighed inwardly, and her patience was severely tested as her dark glance swept him from head to foot. 'It won't be the first time I've laid eyes on a man's bare chest, Mr Boshoff, so take off your shirt and let's have no more nonsense.'

'I don't take my shirt off for no woman except my wife, and you——'

'Having problems, Dr Neal?' a deep, cynical voice enquired, and Jessica turned abruptly to find a pair of cool grey eyes assessing her in a way that sent a peculiar sensation quivering through her which she resented instantly.

Tall, lean and muscular, he stood with his hand resting lightly on the handle of the door and, whoever he was, he exuded an aura of masculinity which was like a force enveloping her before she had time to erect a barricade, and she was almost too afraid to breathe as she continued to stare at him. Dark-haired, and dressed in an exquisitely cut grey suit, he possessed an authoritative manner which instilled something more than just ordinary respect, she realised as she disengaged herself from his magnetism.

Her observations had taken place in no more than the flash of a second before she heard herself explain with surprising calmness, 'I want to examine Mr Boshoff, but he refuses to remove his shirt.'

'She's a woman, Dr Trafford,' the man protested, and Jessica had difficulty in suppressing that flicker of interest that swept through her now as she glanced quickly at the man who had ventured no farther than the door even though he seemed to fill the room with his presence.

'She also happens to be a doctor,' Dane Trafford reminded him sternly, 'and she's seen much more than just a man's chest in her time, so don't be a fool, man, and take off your shirt.'

It was an order, not a request, and the hardy farmer obeyed with a muttered, 'I don't know what this world is coming to.'

Dane Trafford left as quietly as he had appeared, and Jessica carried out her examination without any further protest from her patient.

'Well?' Mr Boshoff demanded when she eventually told him he could put his shirt on again. 'What's wrong with me?'

'Your bronchial tubes are severely congested,' Jessica told him in terms he would understand as she resumed her seat behind her desk, and when he had seated himself opposite her, she asked: 'Do you smoke?'

'Yes,' he barked at her.

'How many cigarettes a day?'

'I . . . well, I . . .'

'Come now, Mr Boshoff,' Jessica demanded with growing impatience. 'How many?'

'About sixty, I suppose,' he admitted grudgingly, but

he rallied swiftly with, 'And don't you tell me to stop smoking!'

'I have no intention of telling you to stop smoking, but I am going to ask you to try and cut down on your nicotine intake, and I mean cut it down to at least half,' Jessica told him. 'I'll also prescribe something for you, and then I'd like you to come and see me again in a week's time.'

'I'd rather see Dr O'Brien, or Dr Trafford.'

'As you wish,' Jessica murmured, suppressing an involuntary smile as she wrote out a prescription and handed it to him.

Her smile broadened when the door closed behind him, but there was no time to linger on the amusing side of her job as the next patient was shown in.

When the last patient for that morning had filtered through her hands, she checked the contents of her bag and fastened the catches. She had wanted variety, and she had certainly got it, she thought with intense satisfaction, but her father's disapproving features suddenly swam before her eyes to dampen her enthusiasm.

The sound of a firm step behind her made her turn, and once again she found herself facing Dane Trafford, but on this occasion he was not content with remaining in the doorway, and he approached her where she stood beside her desk to make her aware not only of his incredible height, but of those pale grey eyes which seemed to miss nothing, not even the faint tightening of her lips. She wrenched her eyes from his and her glance travelled over his superbly chiselled features as she guessed his age somewhere in the mid-thirties, and she decided, at once, that he was much too attractive for his own good.

'Introductions are rather superfluous at the moment, thanks to old James Boshoff,' he remarked, his narrowed glance taking in her appearance now with a slow deliberation from the top of her dark, curly head down to the serviceable shoes on her small feet, and his look filled her with an odd vulnerability and an awareness of her own femininity that made her move her shoulders uncomfortably beneath her white jacket.

'I'd like to thank you, Dr Trafford, for your assistance,' she said, but her voice sounded stilted and unlike her own.

He shrugged casually, but those pale grey eyes remained watchful. 'I dare say you'll help me out some time in a moment of need.'

Was it her imagination, or did she detect an undertone of sensuality in his voice that suggested that he was referring to a personal and not a professional need? Fighting down the unfamiliar wave of heat that invaded her body, she chose to ignore her suspicions.

'Considering that we shall be working together for the next twelve months, my professional assistance will always be at your disposal,' she announced stiffly.

'That's comforting to know,' he smiled cynically, and she knew suddenly that her suspicions had been correct.

She stared a long way up into those mocking grey eyes, telling herself that this man was no different from any other man she had met before in her life, but she knew that this was not so. No man had ever succeeded in making her so intensely aware of the fact that she was a woman, and it was this disquieting thought that made her turn from him to hide her confusion just as Peter O'Brien entered the room.

'Ah, Dane,' Peter's smiling voice swept away some of that odd tenseness which was gripping Jessica. 'I see you've met our new colleague.'

'We have met, yes,' Dane replied coolly, his disturbing gaze roaming over Jessica once again.

'Good,' Peter said brusquely, then he glanced enquiringly from one to the other. 'Has everything gone smoothly this morning?'

'Very smoothly, I should say,' Dane told him, smiling faintly in Jessica's direction in a way that made her recall vividly those awkward moments with James Boshoff, and his manner angered her for some reason.

'Any calls, Sister Hansen?' Peter asked as Emily entered the room in her brisk manner to collect the patient's files on Jessica's desk.

'Not one,' Emily Hansen shook her head, her smile embracing them all. 'You can go home to a quiet lunch for a change.'

'That's the best news I've heard in a long time,' Dane sighed, flexing his wide shoulders, then those compelling grey eyes sought Jessica's. 'Will you join me?'

Play it cool, Jessica warned herself, and her expression somehow mirrored none of her feelings as she asked with pretended innocence, 'For lunch, you mean?'

'Naturally,' he said, his eyes mocking and berating her simultaneously for being a coward.

'Thank you, no,' she declined politely but firmly. 'I still have a few things to sort out before I can say I've settled completely into my new home.'

'Pity,' he shrugged nonchalantly. 'See you all later.'

His long, lithe strides took him swiftly from that room and out of the building, but it was not until his car roared down the street a few moments later that Emily Hansen spoke.

'I'll say one thing for Dr Trafford. He never lets the grass grow under his feet where something in a skirt is concerned, but all the same he's undeniably an excellent doctor.'

Peter O'Brien's expression seemed to hover somewhere between a frown and a smile. 'Between my wife and yourself, Sister Hansen, you're going to make Jessica believe that we're harbouring a ladykiller in our midst.'

'Oh, no!' Sister Hansen not only looked but sounded shocked. 'Dr Trafford isn't a ladykiller, but he has that certain something that definitely makes him irresistible to women.'

'Sex appeal, Sister Hansen?' Peter queried with a wicked smile, and Emily Hansen, for all her years as a nursing Sister, went pink to the roots of her hair.

'Oh, go home to your lunch, both of you,' she laughed heartily, and Jessica and Peter grinned at each other as she marched out of the office.

Jessica had barely swallowed down a sandwich and a cup of tea when the telephone rang shrilly, and when she lifted the receiver Emily Hansen's brisk voice sounded in her ear.

'I apologise for interrupting your lunch hour, Dr Neal, but Dr Trafford has already left for the hospital, and Dr O'Brien is unfortunately on duty in the consulting-rooms this afternoon.'

'What's the problem, Sister Hansen?' Jessica asked with equal briskness, picking up the pencil she had left next to the notepad on the small table.

'I have a call here from Oom Hennie Delport who owns the general dealers in town,' Emily Hansen explained. 'His wife collapsed at their home a few minutes ago, and she's apparently in terrible pain.'

'I'll go at once if you'll give me a few directions.'

'You can't miss their shop in the main street. It's right next door to Logan's bookshop and stationers. The Delport house is in the side street just behind the store.'

Jessica had no difficulty in following Sister Hansen's directions, and within less than ten minutes she was hurrying up the path of the Delport home. The front door opened before she had time to knock, and she introduced herself hastily.

'I'm Dr Neal, Mr Delport.'

'Yes, yes ... come this way.' He stepped aside and Jessica followed his thin, bony frame down the passage. 'I made her lie down, and I filled a hot water bottle for her, but it doesn't seem to be helping for the pain.'

He gestured Jessica into an airy bedroom where a plump, grey-haired woman reclined on the old-fashioned double bed, and from the greyness of her pallor she was suffering considerable agony.

'Hello, Mrs Delport. I'm Dr Neal,' Jessica smiled down at her as she deposited her bag on the chair beside the bed.

'You don't look like a doctor,' the woman complained goodnaturedly. 'You're much too young, *kindjie*.'

Jessica's hackles would have risen if anyone else had dared to call her a child, but coming from this woman it sounded more like a friendly compliment.

'You will allow me to examine you all the same, won't you?'

'Anything, *kindjie*,' the woman gasped. '*Anything*, just as long as you can do something to take away this pain.'

'You may stay, if you like, Mr Delport,' Jessica told the thin, grey-haired man who seemed to hover with indecision at the foot of the bed, and then she proceeded with a thorough examination of the woman lying on the bed.

Jessica's small, clever hands gently probed the areas around the woman's abdomen, her brain functioning to its fullest capacity as she questioned her patient quietly, and listened intently to the symptoms given.

'How long have you been experiencing these pains, Mrs Delport?'

'Tante Maria,' the woman corrected at once, allowing Jessica to help her straighten her clothes after the examination had been completed. 'Everybody calls me Tante Maria, and my husband there is Oom Hennie.' She pointed to the man seating himself gingerly on the foot of the bed, then she returned her attention to Jessica. 'I've had this pain for a few weeks now. It would come and go, but today was the worst it's ever been.'

Tante Maria continued to speak, trying to minimise her suffering, but Jessica's keen eyes detected signs of lingering pain. 'You didn't think to see a doctor about it before?'

'*Ag*, no! I thought it was indigestion, and I never worried about it.' There was a brief, troubled silence, then her eyes met Jessica's. 'What is it, *kindjie*? What's wrong with me?'

'I can't say for sure, Tante Maria, but I suspect that it might be gallstones.'

'Gallstones?' She spat out the word with a look of such disgust on her face that it brought a smile to Jessica's lips. 'But what will I be doing with gallstones?' the woman demanded indignantly.

'They form in the gall bladder, Tante Maria, but I'm not going to tire you with the medical details at this moment,' Jessica told her patient calmly while she opened her bag and prepared a syringe. 'I'm going to give you something for the pain, and then I would like you to go into hospital for a few days.'

'Hospital?' Tante Maria repeated, too surprised at that moment to protest when Jessica rolled her over and bared her buttock to jab the needle into her flesh.

'I would like you to be X-rayed. In that way we can make sure that my diagnosis is correct, and after that we can decide what's to be done,' Jessica explained calmly.

'But I can't go to hospital, Doctor,' Tante Maria protested loudly the moment she was respectable again. 'What will happen to Hennie while I'm lying there high and dry?'

'I'll manage, Maria. Don't you worry about me,' Oom Hennie spoke for the first time, and his voice was firm and reassuring to Tante Maria as well as Jessica. 'It's all right, Doctor, I'll take her to the hospital at once.'

Jessica nodded. 'I'll make the necessary arrangements that end.'

Moments later, when she slid behind the wheel of her biscuit-coloured Alfa, Jessica found herself facing a problem. During the course of the morning Emily Hansen had informed her that there were only three prominently visible buildings in Louisville. The one was the stone church, which Jessica already knew, and the other two served as the local school and hospital. Both were clearly visible as Jessica drove down the main street, but the problem was which one was which.

There was no luck involved, however, in finding the hospital. There were signposts clearly indicating the way to someone like herself who was a stranger to Louisville, and ten minutes later she was entering the cool, air-conditioned building which was surrounded by tall pines and shady mopane trees.

Never having had much to do with the administrative side of her profession in the past, Jessica glanced about her with a degree of uncertainty.

'Well, look what we have here,' Dane Trafford's mocking voice remarked behind her, and for the third time that day she found herself facing this man who seemed curiously intent upon shattering her composure as well as her confidence.

'You look a little lost, if I may say so,' he remarked dryly, his firm yet sensuous mouth curving cynically at the corners as he observed her from his great height.

'I am ... a little,' she was forced to admit. 'I'd like to make arrangements for a patient to be admitted this afternoon, and I want her to be X-rayed as soon as possible.'

'Follow me, Dr Neal,' he gestured mockingly, and she was intensely aware of his tall, muscular frame in the white hospital coat as she accompanied him down a wide passage to the offices of those who were in charge of admittances. 'Who is your patient?'

'Mrs Delport,' she replied to his casual query.

'Tante Maria?' He glanced at her in quick surprise, dark brows raised above keen grey eyes. 'Good heavens, she's always had the constitution of an ox. What's the matter with her?'

'I suspect gallstones.'

'Hm . . . nasty,' he muttered, pausing outside the door marked 'admission', and once again that hint of cynicism touched his mouth. 'You're sure it's gallstones?'

'Ninety-nine per cent sure, yes,' Jessica replied, adding sarcastically, 'Do you doubt my diagnostic capabilities, Dr Trafford?'

His straight dark brows rose a fraction higher above those mocking eyes. 'Far be it from me to doubt your diagnosis, Dr Neal, but it could be that it's merely a digestive complaint.'

'I'm pretty sure it isn't.'

Her voice was brittle with suppressed anger, and without giving him the opportunity to say more, she knocked and entered the office, closing the door firmly behind her. Dane Trafford was the most infuriating man she had ever had the misfortune to meet, she decided, but this was not the moment to make a mental list of the things she was beginning to dislike about him.

With the necessary arrangements finally made, Jessica walked back the way she had come, but the sound of footsteps behind her sent a peculiar sensation shivering up her spine.

'Dr Neal,' that now familiar, mocking voice stopped her in her stride, and she turned with an inward sigh to face the tall, imposing figure approaching her with such lithe, almost athletic strides. 'If you don't mind playing carrier pigeon, I have a set of X-rays I'd like you to take along to Peter. He's rather anxious to take a look at them.'

'Certainly, Dr Trafford.'

'Oh, and Dr Neal?' he stopped her again after the large

brown envelope had exchanged hands. 'If you would like a second opinion on Tante Maria, my services are at your disposal.'

Jessica steeled herself before she turned again to face him, and with a coolness in her smile which he could not avoid noticing, she said caustically, 'That's very kind of you, Dr Trafford, but I don't happen to be in any doubt.'

'There speaks the voice of professional confidence,' he mocked her openly now, and, for some reason she could not even explain to herself, she found herself on the defensive.

'How am I to expect my patients to have confidence in me if I don't have the necessary confidence in myself?'

'True, true,' he muttered in that derisive tone of voice he had used before, and it was with the greatest difficulty that she suppressed the angry words that sprang to her lips.

'Was there anything else, Dr Trafford?' she asked instead.

'Not that I can think of, unless you would consent to dine with me this evening?' he challenged.

Mentally winded, she could think of nothing to say for one startled moment, but she recovered her composure swiftly, and replied with equal smoothness, 'I'm sure you'll find someone else more entertaining with whom you could occupy your free time, Dr Trafford.'

'No doubt I shall,' he assured her mockingly, and as they parted company she once again had the feeling that, because she had failed to meet his challenge, he had branded her a coward.

Shrugging off this uncomfortable thought, she climbed into her Alfa and drove back to the consulting-rooms where she waded once again through a variety of patients.

One of these, however, she had cause to remember. A brief glance at the file on her desk had given her the information that the patient's name was Olivia King, and it also mentioned that her age was twenty-nine, but it was not until the woman herself walked into the room that Jessica found herself looking at her with more than her usual keenness.

Olivia King was small, no taller than Jessica, with silky auburn hair falling softly about her finely etched features, and she was quite obviously in the last stages of pregnancy. Thick, dark lashes framed expressive grey eyes, and the wide, faintly vulnerable mouth suggested a tender, compassionate nature. Her warm, friendly smile was contageous, and Jessica found herself smiling back at her without hesitation.

'Good afternoon, Mrs King,' she greeted her. 'Won't you sit down?'

'Thank you,' Olivia King sighed, lowering herself thankfully into the chair Jessica had indicated.

'You're actually Dr O'Brien's patient, according to this file,' Jessica observed, glancing at the papers before her.

'That's correct,' Olivia King acknowledged, unmistakable mischief dancing in her eyes. 'When I heard that the new doctor was a woman I told him I'd much rather see you in future.'

Jessica laughed shortly. 'I'm honoured, Mrs King.'

'Honoured?'

The woman looked startled, her grey eyes questioning, and Jessica found herself explaining, 'Most of my patients this morning, with the exception of a few, were rather reluctant to have a woman treat their ailments, but here at last I have someone who has specifically asked to see me.'

'Actually,' Olivia King confided guiltily, 'I've been afraid all along that Peter might feel insulted if I went to see someone else instead of him, but your being a woman has given me the excuse I needed.'

'I'm afraid I don't quite understand,' Jessica frowned

slightly. 'Why should you need an excuse to change your doctor?'

'Vivien, Peter's wife, is my husband's sister.' That guilty smile hovered about her lips once more. 'So, you see, it's been rather awkward.'

'I suppose it has,' Jessica agreed amiably before casting a professional glance in her patient's direction. 'Are you here for a general check-up?'

'Yes, I am.'

'Would you just slip out of your clothes and put on that robe, Mrs King?' Jessica suggested. 'I'll be back in a few minutes to examine you.'

Jessica went into the adjoining room to attend to a little boy with a deep cut on his finger, but, when she returned, she found Olivia King waiting patiently for the examination to begin.

'You haven't much longer to go, I don't think,' Jessica remarked at length when she had completed her examination.

'I hope no longer than another ten days,' Olivia smiled dreamily, allowing Jessica to assist her off the high bunk.

Jessica returned to her desk to make the necessary notes in the file before her, and she looked eventually to see Olivia King seat herself in the chair on the other side of her desk.

'This is your first child, so I presume you're excited?' Jessica remarked conversationally.

'I am, yes,' Olivia nodded, 'and I'm a little nervous.'

'You have nothing to worry about.'

'So Peter has told me often enough, but I do worry all the same,' Olivia laughed selfconsciously. 'I'm nearly thirty, and I've heard so many stories about women of my age having problems when it's time for the baby to be born.'

Jessica smiled wryly as she put down her pen and leaned back in her chair. 'Why is it, I wonder, that some people are so fond of scaring the hell out of others?'

'There'll always be people like that as long as there are fools like myself to pay attention to them,' Olivia replied with an equally wry smile, then her expression sobered, and her large grey eyes grew misty with emotion. 'I want this baby very much.'

'I'm sure you do.'

'It will bind our family more securely than ever. You see ...' Olivia hesitated with a measure of uncertainty, then she plunged into an explanation. 'My husband was a widower with a ten-year-old daughter when I met him, and although we're very close, this baby will unite us even more firmly.'

'Your stepdaughter ... er ... what's her name?'

'Frances.'

'Is Frances excited about acquiring a brother or a sister?'

'Almost uncontrollably excited,' Olivia King replied, concern written all over her face. 'That's one of the reasons I'm so afraid something might go wrong.'

'Nothing will go wrong if I can possibly help it, so please don't worry unduly,' Jessica assured her, and a smile hovered on her lips as she allowed her clinical glance to slide over the woman seated before her. 'You're small, like myself, but I'm willing to bet that you're deceptively strong.'

'I feel much better already just talking to you,' Olivia sighed. 'I hope you'll come out to the farm some day soon for a visit, and not in your professional capacity?'

'That's very kind of you, Mrs King.'

'My name is Olivia,' she smiled warmly. 'As Vivien told me once shortly after my arrival in Louisville, here we're all like one big family, and that's truly how it is.'

'Thank you, Olivia,' Jessica murmured, 'and please call me Jessica.'

'I hope you'll be happy here among us, Jessica. The

people are wonderful once you get to know them,' Olivia told her as she rose from her chair. 'And now I really must go.'

'I'd like to see you again in a week's time,' Jessica reminded her.

'Of course.' Olivia flashed her a smile. 'And thank you for giving me so much of your time.'

'That's part of my job, Olivia, to listen to my patients.'

Olivia nodded. 'I'll see you next week, then, if not sooner.'

The door closed behind her, and for some time Jessica found herself staring at it with a peculiar feeling in her breast. Olivia King was a small, generous creature who possessed a certain charm and warmth which one could not avoid noticing. Her warmth had touched Jessica that afternoon, and it had somehow left her enriched.

CHAPTER THREE

JESSICA went to the hospital after dinner that evening to see Tante Maria Delport, and found her lying propped up against the pillows, waiting for the visiting hour when her husband would be paying her a visit.

'Hello, *kindjie*,' Tante Maria smiled when she looked up to see Jessica approaching her bed, then a frown settled between her blue eyes. 'What *is* your name, Dr Neal?'

'Jessica.'

'Well, look here, Jessica,' the older woman began a little irritably. 'The pain is gone, and I'm feeling much better. Couldn't I go home now to Oom Hennie?'

'I'm afraid that's out of the question, Tante Maria,' Jessica shook her dark head firmly. 'You don't have any pain now because I've prescribed something for it, and I've arranged for you to be X-rayed tomorrow.'

'I know what you doctors are like,' Tante Maria grumbled. 'Once you get a poor soul like me into hospital, you won't let me out until you have had a chance to put your knife into me.'

Jessica fingered the old woman's pulse and smiled. 'If we have to operate, then it will be for your own good.'

'I know, *kindjie*, and if I sound as if I'm complaining then it's because I'm worried about my old man. I miss him.'

'I'm sure he's missing you too,' Jessica said gently, 'but it won't be for ever.'

Tante Maria nodded, but her glance suddenly travelled beyond Jessica. 'Here comes that nice Dr Trafford,' she said and, smiling up at Jessica, she added, 'Isn't he handsome?'

Jessica's back stiffened automatically. 'I wouldn't really know.'

'You wouldn't really know what, Dr Neal?' that mocking voice demanded before his tall, muscular frame entered Jessica's line of vision to take up position on the opposite side of the high bed, and his presence made her feel uneasy.

'We were having a private discussion, Dr Trafford,' Jessica replied swiftly before Tante Maria might decide to enlighten him.

'Ah, so it's secrets you've been whispering into Tante Maria's ear, is it?' His mocking glance slid from Jessica to the woman who was observing them with a certain degree of curiosity. 'You will tell me everything when Dr Neal is not around, won't you, Tante Maria?'

'I'll tell you nothing, you scoundrel,' Tante Maria announced, but the smile in her eyes belied the severity in her voice.

'Now is that the way for my best girl to talk to me?' Dane Trafford demanded with an injured look on his tanned face.

'You're lucky I don't clip you one on the ear sometimes,' Tante Maria laughed.

'You've crushed my ego, my dear Tante.'

'Never mind your ego, Dane Trafford,' Tante Maria began reprovingly, taking one of his strong, capable-looking hands and clasping it between her own. 'When are you going to find yourself a nice woman you can settle down with?'

A cynical smile lurked instantly about his firm mouth. 'Find me a nice, gentle woman like yourself, Tante Maria, and I'll marry her tomorrow.'

'I'll do nothing of the kind,' the old woman protested indignantly. 'You've got eyes in your head to help you find one for yourself, but you won't find her while you're staring blindly in the wrong direction.'

Having heard about the woman who was supposedly Dane Trafford's mistress, Jessica held her breath, but he merely laughed shortly, and said casually, 'Perhaps I enjoy the direction I'm staring in.'

'Then you have my sympathy,' Tante Maria almost snapped at him.

Dane Trafford shook his sleek, dark head, and there was a surprising glint of humour in those grey eyes as he looked down upon the woman lying on the bed. 'I don't know why I allow you to talk to me like this.'

'It's because I happen to be old enough to be your mother, and besides . . .' Tante Maria paused and smiled up at him warmly, 'I'm fond of you even though you're such a rascal.'

Jessica was beginning to feel like an intruder and, clearing her throat, she said: 'I'll see you again tomorrow, Tante Maria.'

'All right, Jessica.'

'Just a minute, Dr Neal.' An authoritative hand was raised to prevent her from leaving, and she was forced to wait while Dane Trafford took his leave of Tante Maria. A few minutes later, as they walked down the wide passage towards the lift, he glanced at Jessica speculatively. 'They serve excellent coffee here in the canteen.'

'That's nice,' Jessica replied coolly as they stepped into the lift and were swept down to the ground floor, 'but it's late, and I'd like to go home.'

'That's a good idea,' he nodded, a look of the devil in his eyes that made her heart leap wildly with something close to fear. 'I'm sure you would make an even better cup of coffee.'

Jessica glanced at him sharply. 'That wasn't an invitation.'

'Of course it was,' he argued smoothly as the lift doors opened and, following her out of the building into the well-lit parking area, he added arrogantly, 'I invited myself.'

She stopped abruptly and looked up at him with fury in her eyes. 'If you think I——'

'I'll follow you in my car, and don't speed,' he interrupted warningly. 'They're very strict about speeding here in Louisville.'

His long, lithe strides took him towards the red Mustang parked a little distance from her Alfa, and Jessica fumed inwardly as she slid behind the wheel of her car and inserted the key into the ignition. Just what was all this leading up to? she wondered furiously as she reversed out of the parking space and rammed the lever into a forward gear. If Dane Trafford had intentions of amusing himself with her while his girl-friend was out of reach in Pretoria, then he could think again. She wanted nothing to do with him! Nothing, that was, except professionally.

He was behind her all the way to the cottage, and he was behind her, too, when she unlocked the door and switched on the lights. His presence was unnerving, and his silent determination more than a little frightening, but she was not going to allow herself to be intimidated, or influenced by him.

'Hm . . . nice,' he said, following her into the kitchen as if he expected her to dart out the back door in an effort to escape him. 'Did you know that this was Peter's consulting-rooms when he started up his practice here in Louisville?'

Jessica switched on the electric kettle and her hands trembled ridiculously as she spooned instant coffee into the cups. 'So Vivien told me.'

'Ah, Vivien,' he replied with a hint of sardonic humour in his voice. 'That lady doesn't altogether approve of me.'

'You know why, of course,' Jessica replied without turning.

'Do you?'

His query was abrupt and unexpected, just as her

remark had been uncalled for, but for some inexplicable reason she had been unable to prevent herself from taking that little dig at him.

'How do you like your coffee?' she asked, changing the subject.

'Strong, black, and without sugar.' He was standing directly behind her when she switched off the kettle and poured the water into the cups. 'And you never answered my question.'

'Your personal life is none of my concern, Dr Trafford.'

Sensuous fingers trailed lightly across her shoulder to the nape of her neck, and a warm, electrifying current surged through her to set her nerves vibrating in the most alarming manner.

'You could make it your concern, Jessica,' he suggested, using her name with ease, and his deep voice mocked and caressed simultaneously, but Jessica had no intention of allowing her control to slip.

Turning, she thrust the cup of steaming liquid into his hands, and there was nothing but cool indifference in her dark eyes when they met his. 'Drink your coffee, Dr Trafford, then I must ask you to leave.'

'Why?' he demanded with an annoying arrogance she was beginning to expect from him.

'I'd like to go to bed.'

'So would I.' Shock, and something else which she could not define, raced through her while she watched him seat himself at the table as if he had intentions of spending the night there. Mocking grey eyes were raised in that instant to meet her startled brown gaze. 'No clever answer this time?'

Pulling herself together sharply, she picked up her own cup of coffee and turned towards the table. 'Your remark doesn't deserve an answer.'

The telephone started ringing before she had the opportunity to sit down, and she went to answer it with a feeling of relief to discover that it was for Dane.

'It's for you,' she said when she had turned to find him entering her lounge, but she could not help overhearing his conversation as she made her way back to the kitchen.

'Yes? . . . Yes? . . . Get him into the theatre at once. I'll be there as quick as I can.'

The conversation ended abruptly, and moments later Dane Trafford was dwarfing the doorway into the kitchen. 'Someone swallowed a chicken bone. If you'd like to come along it would help you become acquainted with the general layout of the hospital for future reference.'

Gone was the Casanova image she had encountered up till now, and in its place was an authoritative, professional man. Confused and bewildered, she snatched up her car keys in silence, and followed him out, leaving two cups of coffee untouched on the kitchen table.

In the theatre, not a half hour later, Jessica watched with growing admiration while those strong hands with the long, sensitive fingers removed the small bone which had lodged dangerously in the patient's trachea. As a physician and surgeon he obviously commanded respect from those who met him in that capacity, and Jessica understood now why most people were so willing to overlook his personal misdemeanours.

Dane stayed on at the hospital to assure himself of his patient's welfare, but he instructed Jessica to return home, and she obeyed without a murmur. It had been a long day full of problems and surprises, and she had a feeling that, despite her father's dubious acceptance of her decision, she was going to enjoy working here among the people of Louisville.

Jessica clipped the X-rays on to the scanner and stepped back to examine them. The obstructions were there, settled firmly in the bile ducts, and thrusting her hands into the pockets of her white jacket, she continued to stare at the X-rays while Tante Maria's statement pivoted through her mind.

'I know what you doctors are like. Once you get a poor soul like me into hospital you won't let me out until you have had a chance to put your knife into me.'

A rueful expression flashed across Jessica's sensitive features. It was going to be just like that for that nice old lady whom she had met only the day before, and there was nothing anyone could do about it.

'Good afternoon.' Jessica jumped visibly. She wished Dane Trafford wouldn't always sneak up on her like this, and there was a flash of anger in her eyes when she turned to glance up at him, but he was looking at the X-rays on the scanner, and not at her. 'Tante Maria's?' he questioned abruptly.

Jessica nodded, and murmured 'Yes', her eyes following the direction of his once more.

'May I compliment you on your accurate diagnosis?'

There was nothing complimentary in his tone of voice, only that hateful mockery, but she parried it with a cool, 'Thank you, Dr Trafford.'

'Would you like me to do the operation?'

'I'm sure I shall manage perfectly,' she replied with a hint of sarcasm behind her smile, 'but if you're in doubt, then I shan't object if you'd like to assist me.'

'I shall look forward to it,' he surprised her with his acceptance, but that sardonic gleam in his eyes lingered for only a moment. 'When are you going to tell her?'

'I'll go and see her now during my lunch hour,' Jessica replied, switching off the light behind the scanner, and returning the X-rays to their envelope. 'I don't think she's going to like it, though.'

'Tante Maria is very much mouth at times, but she's also a sensible woman with plenty of heart.'

'I gathered that,' she nodded thoughtfully, then a sigh escaped her. 'Well, there's no sense in delaying the inevitable, is there?'

'No sense at all,' Dane agreed abruptly. 'Keep me posted, will you?'

'I'll do that,' Jessica promised.

Several minutes later she was standing beside Tante Maria's bed in the women's general ward. Tante Maria did not pretend that she liked the idea of having an operation, but, as Dane had predicted, she took it sensibly.

'If it has to be done, *kindjie*, then I'd be foolish to put up an argument,' she remonstrated after Jessica had broken the news to her. 'All I'd like to know is . . . when?'

'As soon as possible,' Jessica replied. 'Tomorrow, if I can arrange it.'

'That's good,' Tante Maria nodded grimly. 'The sooner it's done, the sooner I can go home.'

There was an awkward little silence which Jessica filled by admiring the hothouse chrysanthemums in the vase beside Tante Maria's bed.

'Olivia brought them this morning,' she told Jessica.

'Olivia King?'

Tante Maria nodded, her eyes lighting up with pleasure. 'She's a lovely young woman, and this town had never seen such a wedding as on the day Olivia married Bernard King.'

'It was a big wedding, then?' Jessica remarked casually, but curiously.

'*Kindjie!*' Tante Maria exclaimed, clasping her hands together against her ample bosom. 'There wasn't place in that old stone church for everyone. Not all of them were invited, of course, but they went all the same, and there was not a woman there that day who did not shed a tear when Olivia entered the church on Peter O'Brien's arm.'

'You're very fond of Olivia,' Jessica observed, not quite sure where all this was leading to, but if it took Tante Maria's mind off the imminency of her operation for a while, then it did not matter.

'Yes, I am fond of her,' Tante Maria admitted. 'Logan's Bookshop belongs to her, and in those days, before she married Bernard, she used to live in the flat above the shop, but that's been changed now, and the flat has now become an extended part of the shop.' Her blue gaze was reminiscent. 'That was three years ago, but it still seems like only yesterday when Olivia arrived here in Louisville, a thin, insecure little thing.'

Jessica smiled faintly. 'She's asked me to do her confinement, did you know that?'

'She told me.' Blue eyes surveyed Jessica intently. 'You remind me a little of her, you know. You're just as small and thin.'

'Don't look at me as though you're contemplating a fattening-up process,' Jessica laughed.

'Even doctors sometimes don't know what's good for them.' Her eyes gazed up at Jessica with a certain amount of sternness in their depths. 'Why aren't you married yet, Jessica?'

Jessica smiled inwardly, but outwardly she maintained a seriousness to match the older woman's expression. 'There hasn't been time to think of marriage.'

'Nonsense!' Tante Maria exclaimed crossly. 'There's always time to think of marriage.'

'When one has met the right man, yes.'

'How do you know that you haven't met him already?' Tante Maria demanded at once while observing Jessica closely.

'I should imagine I would know when I have.'

'That's just where you're wrong,' Tante Maria argued. 'Sometimes you look at a man and you think "He's not right for me at all", and yet, when you get to know him better, you find out that he's the right man after all.'

Jessica was beginning to feel decidedly uncomfortable, for Tante Maria sounded very much like her own mother at that moment. 'The man I marry one day will have to share the same interests as I do.'

'You mean it would have to be someone like Dane Trafford?'

'I hope not like him at all!' Jessica replied at once, her insides recoiling at the thought, but Tante Maria was not finished yet.

'If the right woman came along he would make a good husband,' she insisted, her eyes watchful.

'Well, I'm not that woman,' Jessica stated firmly, and brought the conversation to an end with, 'I suggest that you rest for a while before Oom Hennie pays you a visit this afternoon.'

The curious glances of Tante Maria's fellow patients followed Jessica from the ward as if they had heard every word spoken between them, and, for the first time in some years, Jessica felt a slight warmth stealing into her cheeks.

Dane Trafford good husband material? she thought disparagingly. Never! She would have more in common with a plumber than with a man who looked upon every woman he met as a potential bedmate!

Jessica was too busy that afternoon to give her conversation with Tante Maria further thought, but when she was alone in her cottage that evening, it sneaked into her mind, although she was fortunately capable of laughing it off and forgetting about it. She had something far more important to occupy her thoughts with, and that something was Tante Maria's operation the following morning. Dane Trafford would be assisting her, and she knew perfectly well that he was going to be critical.

Jessica's supposition was correct. When she faced Dane across Tante Maria's prostrate figure on the operating table, his cool, assessing eyes made her feel slightly disconcerted. In green theatre gown and cap, with a white sterile mask covering his nose and mouth, he looked very much like everyone else, and she tried desperately to ignore his presence, but Dane Trafford was not someone you could ignore with ease. She felt very much like a student about to operate for the first time under the watchful eyes of her professor, and it was a damned uncomfortable feeling. Her confidence plunged to a dangerously low level, and it was at this point that the anaesthetist indicated that the operation could begin.

With a silent prayer in her heart Jessica held out her hand, and her confidence came flooding back from the moment the first instrument was slapped into her gloved palm. Dane Trafford was there, but he no longer posed a threat to her, and she worked on steadily with an efficiency her own critical mind could not fault.

'That was neatly done, Dr Neal,' Dane Trafford remarked when, at last, they had discarded their theatre garb and were enjoying a welcome cup of tea in the doctors' rest-room which was situated close to the theatre. Jessica looked up, gratified that he should compliment her, but what followed was nothing of the kind. 'One thing I must say for women doctors,' he said dryly, 'they usually make a much neater job of sewing up a patient than a man—but then needlework comes easy to women.'

An angry nerve pulsed against her temple, but she controlled herself at once, determined not to be rattled by him. 'Is that your way of telling me that you didn't approve of the way I performed the operation itself?'

Straight dark brows rose fractionally above mocking grey eyes. 'There's room for improvement, I must admit.'

'Thank you, Dr Trafford,' she smiled sarcastically. 'That's most encouraging.'

'What I'm getting at, Dr Neal, is that a man approaches an operation differently from a woman,' he explained, commanding her unwilling attention. 'To a man that patient on the operating table is just another patient, but to a woman it's a totally different matter. I'm not saying that women don't make good surgeons or doctors, but they do have the tedious habit of becoming emotionally involved with their patients, and that not only clouds their judgment, but it hampers their work.'

'You think so?'

'I don't only think it, I know it,' he replied, ignoring that hint of sarcasm in her voice. 'You hated having to cut into Tante Maria.'

'Your notions about women in the medical field are archaic, but I'll admit that I dislike having to cut into anyone unless it's absolutely necessary,' she felt forced to defend herself. 'I've known too many people with parts of their body yanked out unnecessarily because of a knife-happy surgeon.'

A strong, long-fingered hand gestured in a dismissive manner. 'I won't argue with you in that respect, but it's your capabilities as a surgeon that we're discussing.'

Jessica placed her empty cup in the tray and sighed audibly. 'I presume you're going to lecture me on how the operation should have been performed?'

'No,' he smiled derisively. 'I can't fault you on your technique.'

'Really?' she smiled coldly, making no effort to hide the angry sarcasm in her voice.

'It's your approach to surgery that troubles me,' he explained.

'Something tells me that we're right back where we started,' she sighed again, and, before he could open his mouth, she said it for him. 'My approach to surgery is too feminine, and too emotional.'

'Precisely.'

'I disagree with you, and I'm afraid I can't change the fact that I'm a woman,' she announced sharply, rising to her feet in the hope of ending the conversation, but Dane Trafford had not finished with her yet.

'I would never ask you to change. I happen to like

what I see of the feminine side of Dr Jessica Neal.'

The unexpected sensuality in his voice washed over her like a slow caress and, to her horror, her skin tingled as if he had actually touched her with those clever, supple hands. She raised her glance cautiously, but it was a mistake. Those pale grey eyes were the disturbing eyes of a man who knew women too well, and he must surely be aware of the response he was awakening in her.

'I'm going to take a last look at Tante Maria before I have a word with Oom Hennie,' she announced, her voice abrupt with the effort to control the unfamiliar and unwanted sensations she was experiencing.

'Does it embarrass you to think that I should see you as a woman rather than a doctor, Jessica?' he asked, using her name with that familiar ease which merely enhanced the sensations she was trying so desperately to suppress, and a spark of resentment flared within her when she suspected that he knew exactly what he was doing to her.

'Not at all, Dr Trafford,' she replied untruthfully, 'and I know that my mother would be thrilled to learn that I haven't lost my femininity entirely by choosing to become a doctor.'

He was beside her in an instant, moving with the silent swiftness of a panther, and his fingers snaked about her wrist before she could reach the door. She stood perfectly still, determined to remain calm, but his touch once again sent that warm, electrifying current surging through her that set her nerves vibrating at his nearness.

'Given half a chance I could prove to you just how feminine you really are.'

'I don't doubt your capabilities in that respect,' she replied with a forced casualness, hoping he could not feel the throbbing of her pulse beneath his fingertips as she disengaged her wrist from his clasp and moved away from his oddly disturbing nearness to add carelessly, 'The problem is I have no desire to find out just how capable you are.'

A frown of irritation had settled between her winged brows as she made her way towards Tante Maria's ward, but her irritation was directed at herself. She had always prided herself on having firm control over her emotions, but Dane Trafford had a way of piercing her armour, and it was this alarming knowledge that disturbed her so intensely. She would have to take greater care in future not to tangle with him unnecessarily, but having to work with him made her realise just how impossible that was going to be.

Jessica had been in Louisville just over a week when James Boshoff was shown into her consulting-room late one afternoon, and she had great difficulty in suppressing her smile of amusement when he approached her desk with that sweaty, wide-brimmed hat clutched in his rough hands.

'Good afternoon, Mr Boshoff,' she said politely. 'I thought you would be seeing Dr O'Brien, or Dr Trafford.'

'Yes, well, I . . .' He lowered his glance a little sheepishly. 'I thought I'd come and tell you, Doctor, that the medicine you prescribed for me has helped, and I'm also smoking much less now.'

'I'm very glad to hear that,' Jessica replied, gesturing him into the chair on the other side of her desk.

There was an uncomfortable little silence, then he cleared his throat before speaking. 'Maria Delport talks of nothing else but how good you were to her, and she's looking so much better.'

'Tante Maria has been a very good patient,' Jessica announced, realising with some embarrassment that Tante Maria had done her own particular brand of campaigning among the people of Louisville.

'Did you want to examine me again, Doctor?'

'Yes, Mr Boshoff,' Jessica nodded, smothering a smile at his willingness on this occasion to be examined by her.

'Remove your shirt and make yourself comfortable on that stool.'

The examination did not last long, and as she removed her stethoscope from about her neck and placed it on her desk, he asked anxiously, 'I am better, aren't I, Doctor?'

'Yes, Mr Boshoff,' she nodded, seating herself and making the necessary notes in his file before she looked up to find him dressed and hovering beside her desk. 'You should still have some of the medicine left which I prescribed for you, so I would like you to continue taking it, and if you could keep the amount of cigarettes you smoke down to a minimum, then I see no reason why your lungs shouldn't clear up altogether.'

'Thank you, Doctor.' The admiration that shone out of his eyes was almost embarrassing. 'Do you want to see me again?'

'Only if your condition doesn't improve,' she told him, and when she was confronted with his toothy smile, she could no longer suppress her own.

'*Tot siens*, Doctor,' he said, and moments later she was alone in the room with a foolish giggle threatening to burst from her lips.

'So the old fool came back for more of that feminine touch, did he?'

Jessica looked up sharply to see Dane Trafford approaching her desk, and she was struck once again by that powerful aura of virile masculinity which surrounded him. Muscles rippled beneath his white silk shirt, and cream-coloured pants clung to lean hips and muscular thighs. He was a superb example of male physical fitness, but the root of the trouble was that she was finding it increasingly difficult to observe him from a clinical point of view. She looked up suddenly into those grey, mocking eyes, and realised that he was well aware of her interest as he waited for her to reply to his remark.

'I guess Mr Boshoff has realised that I'm not such a bad doctor after all,' she said distractedly, a faint smile lurking about her mouth.

'If I were James Boshoff my reasons for coming back would have nothing to do with your professional capabilities.'

As always the sensuality in his voice, and the suggested intimacy of his remark, brought her to her senses. The smile froze on her lips and, rising abruptly to her feet, she said sharply, 'I think I'd like to go home.'

'Not so fast, Jessica.' He barred her way effectively by stepping in her path. 'We've received a call from one of the farms in the district. A labourer has injured himself, and they're too afraid to move him for fear of back injury. Peter thinks it's a good idea if you go out there with me. It would give you an opportunity to get to know the area around Louisville.'

Her hopes of spending a long, leisurely evening at home were rudely dashed and, sighing inwardly, she slipped out of her white jacket and pushed her stethoscope into her bag.

'Shall we go, then, Dr Trafford?'

He nodded abruptly and informed her in a clipped voice, 'We'll go in my car.'

Ten minutes later the red Mustang was churning up the dust as it sped along the road through the bushveld while the late afternoon sun cast long shadows across the earth. Jessica sat in silence, not interrupting while Dane explained where they were going, and she made mental notes as he pointed out several farms to her.

'The wealthiest cattle farmer in this district is naturally Vivien O'Brien's brother, Bernard King, but his farm lies to the north of Louisville,' Dane explained. 'Around these parts he's known fondly as the Cattle King.'

Jessica did not comment on this, but she could not help thinking that, in the face of what she had just discovered,

Vivien O'Brien and Olivia King had somehow managed to remain two unassuming and lovely people.

Dane turned off on to a bumpy farm road, and when he brought his car to a halt close to a farm shed there was a stirring among the group of people who stood gathered there. A burly farmer stepped from the circle of black faces to explain what had occurred, and they discovered that one of his labourers had slipped and fallen from the roof of the high shed.

Dane and Jessica worked quickly while the light was still reasonably good, examining and assessing the extent of the man's injuries. They worked like a team, strangely enough, and there was no need for further explanations when Dane looked up to say, 'Call the hospital. Tell them to send out an ambulance, and explain what we'll need.'

Jessica nodded and, with the burly farmer leading the way to his house, she was speaking to the hospital a few minutes later.

The labourer's injuries were serious, Jessica realised, but how serious they would only discover once he had been X-rayed, but the external examination had led her to believe that he suffered a dangerous pressure on a vital nerve in the cervix of the spine, and the look on Dane's face when she rejoined him made her suspect that his diagnosis was the same as hers.

The ambulance arrived just as the shadows of night deepened across the veld, and the silent group of inquisitive and concerned observers dispersed at last as the patient was lifted into the vehicle.

'Do you think you could manage to drive my car back into town?' Dane queried, and when she nodded affirmatively, he dropped a small bunch of keys into her outstretched palm. 'See you at the hospital, then.'

He leapt into the ambulance and the doors were slammed shut. Moments later she stood watching the ambulance making its way back to the hospital.

Jessica followed a little while later in Dane's Mustang, and she enjoyed the feeling of being in control of such a powerful car. The stars were glittering in the dark, velvety sky when at last she drove through the gates of the hospital, but there was no time to enjoy it as she parked the car and hurried into the building.

'How is he?' Jessica was asking Dane some minutes later.

'He's being X-rayed at the moment,' he said, shrugging himself into his jacket and combing his fingers through his dark, windblown hair.

'What do you think?'

'Without sounding a little premature, I think that, with luck and care, he'll be walking about in the not too distant future.' His smile was twisted as he glanced at her. 'What do you think?'

'I think he was lucky that everyone had the foresight not to move him until we arrived.'

Dane nodded, then a gleam of speculation settled in his eyes. 'The X-rays will take some time. Will you join me in the canteen for a cup of coffee?'

An involuntary smile tugged at the corners of her mouth. 'I don't seem to have much option, do I?'

'Not unless you fancy walking all the way to the consulting-rooms to collect your car,' he answered smoothly, and she sighed resignedly.

'I'll join you for that cup of coffee.'

'I knew you would accept,' he mocked her, taking her arm to guide her towards the canteen, and she was again made aware of Dane Trafford in the physical sense.

She could not decide whether she liked it, or not, but she was beginning to sense danger for herself in a closer relationship with this man who had such an odd effect on her usually stable emotions.

CHAPTER FOUR

'As I recall,' Dane began, a cynical smile curving his perfectly chiselled mouth when they sat facing each other across the table with a steaming cup of coffee in front of them, 'the last time we had coffee together neither of us had the opportunity to take even one sip.'

Against her will Jessica heard herself laughing. 'I could do with this cup of coffee, so let's hope we have the opportunity now to finish it before we're called away.'

'I echo that wish,' he sighed, and she was surprised to see the lines of weariness etched along the sides of his nose and mouth as they sat drinking their coffee in the partially empty canteen. 'What made you decide to study medicine, Jessica?'

The question startled her, and she gestured vaguely with her hands. 'What makes *anyone* decide to study medicine?'

'I can think of various reasons, but not necessarily the right ones.' His face looked grim. 'I decided to become a doctor when I found myself confronted by the sight of my dying parents after they'd been shot down by terrorists on our farm in Zimbabwe. If I'd known then what I know now, I might still have been able to save their lives.' He offered her a cigarette and, when she shook her head, he lit one for himself. 'I was studying pharmacy at the time, but after that I knew I had to alter my plans,' he added.

She realised that her sympathies would be lost on him at that moment. She was not even sure that he would appreciate them, and her brow creased in a thoughtful frown as she studied him closely. 'That must have been at

59

the start of the guerilla warfare in Zimbabwe.'

'If you're trying to work out my age, then I'll save you the trouble,' he laughed mockingly. 'I'm thirty-five.'

'I wasn't——'

'Oh, yes, you were,' he interrupted, his mocking glance taking in the guilty flush that stained her cheeks. 'Now that you know my reasons for becoming a doctor, what about telling me yours?'

Jessica's mouth felt dry, and she took a quick sip of coffee before she replied. 'I can't remember a time when I didn't want to be a doctor.'

'You mean you grew up with the idea, and never stopped to consider something else which might have suited you better?'

For some inexplicable reason she refrained from telling him about her father, and she lowered her gaze as she said: 'I can't think of anything that would have suited me better.'

When she risked looking at him again she found his eyes glittering with mockery and something else which she preferred not to define. 'I can think of something which would suit you admirably in this period of your life, but you wouldn't need a university degree for that.'

'Even if I say that I'm not interested you're going to enlighten me, I'm sure,' she replied a little caustically, watching him blow twin jets of smoke from his nose as he put out his half-smoked cigarette in the ashtray.

'You're right about that,' he said, those compelling eyes probing hers, attempting to invade the most secret recesses of her soul before they travelled slowly, and with a deliberate sensuality in their depths, down to where her small breasts strained against her silk sweater. His glance lingered like a physical caress, and her treacherous body responded in the most diabolical way which his razor-sharp eyes could not miss. 'What would suit you now is a damn good affair,' he enlightened her, his eyes on that frantic little pulse at the base of her throat, and the agitated rise and fall of her breasts.

'What you're really suggesting is an affair with you, I suppose?' she demanded cynically, and his strong white teeth flashed in a mocking smile.

'I'm delighted that you should consider me in that respect.'

'You intended that I should,' she retorted angrily.

'It grieves me that you should misjudge me so.'

Jessica clenched her hands tightly beneath the table. 'It grieves me that I should have to sit here listening to you.'

'*Dr Trafford. Please report to Casualty. Dr Trafford,*' the male voice over the intercom system interrupted their conversation, and they rose to their feet simultaneously.

'What a pity we can't continue this interesting conversation,' he taunted her as they walked out of the canteen, and she flashed him a withering glance that merely served to increase the mockery in his eyes.

The X-rays confirmed their suspicions, and Dane issued rapid instructions before answering Jessica's silent query with, 'There's a neuro-surgeon in Louis Trichardt. I'll consult him first thing in the morning.'

It was late that evening before Dane parked his Mustang alongside Jessica's Alfa and turned in his seat to face her.

'Goodnight, Jessica,' he said to the accompaniment of the crickets in the undergrowth, and his mocking features were clearly visible in the light from the dashboard. 'May I wish you a peaceful, uninterrupted night in your lonely bed.'

'I don't find my bed lonely at all, Dr Trafford,' she assured him stiffly. 'I prefer sleeping alone, quite frankly.'

'You're missing out on a great deal of excitement, Dr Neal.'

'From your point of view, I suppose I am, but that

doesn't bother me at all,' she replied, climbing out of his car and taking her bag with her.

'You'll change your mind yet.'

'Not if I can help it,' she thought furiously, but aloud she said: 'Goodnight, Dr Trafford, and thanks for the lift.'

She could not swear to it, of course, but the sound of mocking laughter seemed to come from the interior of his car moments before he revved the engine and drove away at speed. He was truly the most infuriating man she had ever met, she decided as she dropped her bag on to the passenger seat and slid in behind the wheel of her car. He was so arrogantly sure of himself as a physician as well as a man and, *dammit*, he knew perfectly well that he was capable of making her aware of him as a man more than a physician.

This was more than just a disquieting thought; it was a downright disturbing discovery, and she would most certainly have to do something about it before it was too late.

During the following three weeks Jessica became more fully acquainted with Louisville and its people. She also became acquainted with the ever-changing routine of her work, and the stimulating challenges she had never experienced as a young doctor walking the wards of the general hospital in Johannesburg. If she had ever doubted her decision, then she no longer had any need to feel that she might have made a grave mistake in coming to Louisville.

There was only one problem. *Dane Trafford*. He was annoyingly persistent in his efforts to seduce her mentally. So far, he had not laid an unnecessary hand on her, but she was becoming frighteningly conscious of the fact that she would come off second best if he should switch from mental to physical seduction.

Sighing irritably and tiredly, Jessica swung her car into her driveway. She was looking forward to a quiet night with a good book, but when she saw Vivien coming quickly towards her car she knew somehow that her hopes had been futile.

'It's Olivia,' Vivien explained, her features tight and anxious as she climbed into the car beside Jessica. 'I'll come with you to show you the way out to Mountain View, and I'll explain on the way.'

Jessica did not need the note of urgency in Vivien's well-modulated voice to make her put her foot down hard on the accelerator. Olivia had gone almost three weeks over her due date, and Jessica knew that the long wait had played havoc with her nerves.

'Olivia asked Frances to give you a ring, and the poor child was in quite a panic when she discovered that you had already left the consulting-rooms, so she rang me instead,' Vivien explained as they left the town behind them. 'Bernard is out somewhere hunting down an injured kudu, and Olivia doesn't think he'll arrive home in time to bring her in to the hospital. That's all my niece could tell me, except that Olivia asked you to come out to the farm, and to come quickly.'

Jessica glanced swiftly at the anxious face of her passenger. 'How far do we still have to go?'

'Another five kilometres and we should be there.'

Jessica drove on in silence, taking note of Vivien's gestured indications where she should turn and where to continue on the same road. She had barely parked her car beneath the jacaranda tree in front of the sprawling, thatch-roofed homestead, with its gauzed-in verandah running along the front and west side of the house, when the gauze door opened and slammed shut behind a long-limbed thirteen-year-old girl who sped towards Vivien like a veritable whirlwind with her long, dark pigtails flying out behind her.

'Aunty Viv, I'm so glad you came!' she almost hiccoughed with emotion against her aunt's breast.

'Don't worry, pet,' Vivien spoke soothingly, running a loving hand over the smooth, dark head. 'Dr Neal is here as well, and everything is going to be all right. Just be a good girl and wait out on the verandah until your father comes.'

'But I want to help,' Frances protested, her dark brows knitting together in a frown.

They had, during the course of this conversation, reached the verandah, and at this point Jessica spoke for the first time. 'If I need your help, Frances, I'll call you, and that's a promise.'

The note of authority in her voice was audible, and Frances submitted to it with a grudging, 'Oh, all right, then.'

In Mountain View's spacious master bedroom, they found Olivia lying on the bed, and she looked peculiarly small and lost in its vastness. She turned her head towards the door the moment they entered the room, and some of the anxiety drained from her white, elfin-shaped face.

'I'm so glad you could come, Jessica, and you too, Vivien,' she smiled up at them weakly. 'If I could have managed it, then I would have driven myself in to town and saved you the trip out here.'

'Good heavens, Olivia, that would have been a foolish thing to do,' Vivien exclaimed reprovingly.

'When did it start?' Jessica queried, placing her bag on the plushly carpeted floor and seating herself on the bed beside Olivia.

'To be truthful, it started this morning, I suppose, but I thought it was cramp, and when it went away I was positive it was nothing to get excited about,' Olivia explained guiltily. 'The real thing started a little more than a half hour ago, and——' She broke off sharply, a spasm of pain twisting her features.

'Just relax,' Jessica ordered quietly. 'Breathe deeply and slowly.'

When the contraction subsided, Jessica examined Olivia swiftly, but she had barely completed her examination before Olivia's body was racked with pain once more.

'Oh, dear!' Vivien breathed anxiously. 'What are we going to do?'

'We're going to deliver the baby right here,' Jessica announced calmly, opening up her bag and checking through its contents.

'You say that as if—as if it's going to be s-soon,' Olivia managed haltingly, her anxious grey eyes meeting Jessica's.

'It *is* going to be soon, Olivia, but we still have time to make the necessary preparations,' Jessica smiled down at her.

Vivien and Frances were only too eager to help, and Jessica galvanished them into action with a calmness that inspired confidence, while at the same time seeing to it that Frances stayed out of the room.

'Jessica?' Olivia cried out her name some minutes later, and Jessica was at her side at once.

'Relax,' she ordered gently, wiping the perspiration from Olivia's face. 'Everything's going smoothly.'

'Oh, God! I wish Bernard were here,' Olivia moaned, the beads of perspiration forming rapidly once again on her pale face.

'If he could sprout wings he would be here this very minute, you know that,' Vivien reminded her quietly.

'Yes, I—I know,' Olivia managed, gritting her teeth as yet another spasm of pain tore through her. 'It's just that he—he's so strong, and at this moment I—I need his strength so desperately.'

'Hang on to me, my dear,' Vivien suggested, giving Olivia her hands to cling to,' and leave the rest to Jessica.'

Olivia's baby was born twenty minutes later, a healthy

little boy who protested loudly and indignantly until Jessica wrapped him up warmly and placed him in his mother's waiting arms for a time.

'May I come in now and see the baby?' Frances demanded through the door soon after they had made Olivia and the baby comfortable, and Vivien opened the door at once to let her in.

'Come in, pet,' she smiled at her niece, and the long-limbed child was beside the cradle in an instant, staring down at the baby with something close to awe on her feet.

'He's so tiny,' Frances whispered anxiously. 'Will he grow, Olivia?'

'He'll grow, darling,' Olivia assured Frances tiredly, but her face was aglow with happiness. 'He'll grow to be just as tall as you one day.'

Frances' face lit up with a smile and she embraced Olivia excitedly before turning to face Jessica and Vivien. 'I almost forgot,' she said guiltily. 'Evalina said to tell you there's coffee in the living-room if you'd like some. I'll stay with Olivia while you're gone.'

Vivien seemed to hesitate, but Jessica touched her arm lightly. 'A cup of strong coffee would do us both good.'

Later, in the living-room with its polished furniture and homely atmosphere, Jessica sipped her coffee and came to terms with the knowledge that she would never quite be able to take the miracle of birth for granted. It was something which continued to fill her with awe and silent wonder, and, glancing at Vivien, Jessica suspected that she felt very much the same at the moment.

Vivien looked up suddenly, and with eyes that looked suspiciously bright as if the tears weren't far, she said quietly, 'I grew up on this farm, and in this very house. I've watched animals giving birth, and I've marvelled at it, but today, watching Olivia's baby being born, I feel humbled and terribly insignificant.' She sighed and looked away, but not before Jessica had seen the moisture gathering in her eyes. 'I realise now, more than ever, that I've missed out on the most joyous part of marriage.'

Jessica's throat tightened, but, before she could say anything, Vivien had pulled herself together, and was helping herself to a second cup of coffee.

It was dusk before the silence was disturbed by the sound of a truck roaring up to the house, and Jessica was alone in the room with Olivia and the baby when she heard quick, heavy footsteps coming down the passage.

'Where is she? Where's Olivia?' a deep, thundering voice demanded.

'She's here, Bernard,' Jessica heard Vivien say, 'and there's nothing to worry about.'

Bernard King swore loudly, and there was just enough time for Jessica and Olivia to exchange amused glances before the bedroom door was flung open beneath a heavy, anxious hand.

The man who stood framed in the doorway was incredibly tall, and his dark hair was liberally flecked with grey. The square, jutting jaw and powerfully built body were enough to make Jessica realise that this was not a man to be crossed in anger. His dark, ferocious glance flicked over her with total lack of interest before seeking out the small woman lying propped up against the pillows on the bed, and then something incredible happened. Those hard eyes softened miraculously with a look of tender devotion and, big man though he was, Jessica saw him swallow as if emotion had formed a constriction in his throat.

'Olìvia?' he whispered hoarsely, and then he was kneeling beside the bed, obliterating Olivia's small frame almost completely as he gathered her up against his khaki-clad chest and buried his face against her throat.

Jessica glanced briefly at Vivien, but she was almost

too afraid to move. She was caught up in something indescribably beautiful, and she dared not intervene, nor disturb the moment. Between Bernard and Olivia King there was that something special; that enviable something which most people longed for, but which so few experienced, and Jessica, sensing this, felt an emptiness and a need within herself which she had never known before.

'Forgive us for being so rude, Jessica,' Olivia's voice filtered through to Jessica's conscious mind. 'I'd like you to meet my husband, Bernard. Darling, this is Dr Jessica Neal.'

The large man rose to his feet, and Jessica's hand was taken in a firm, hard grip that made her fingers ache. 'I'm glad to know you, Jessica, and thank you for coming so promptly to Olivia's aid.'

Those dark eyes were smiling now, and as Vivien stepped farther into the room, after remaining silently and discreetly just inside the doorway, Jessica noticed the strong likeness between brother and sister.

'Aren't you going to take a peek at our son?' Olivia wanted to know, and three pairs of eyes watched with mixed expressions as Bernard King leaned over the cradle with a certain amount of indulgence to examine the tiny, wrapped-up bundle that lay there sleeping contentedly.

'He's an ugly little devil,' Bernard observed at last with a twinkle in his eyes.

'Naturally,' Olivia smiled up at him a little cheekily. 'He looks just like his father.'

Bernard laughed softly as he seated himself beside Olivia once more, and his laughter was a low rumble coming from deep within his strong throat. 'I deserved that, didn't I?'

'You certainly did,' Vivien intervened humorously, then she glanced at Jessica who was packing her bag and preparing to leave. 'Peter telephoned and he should be here any minute now, so I'm assured of a lift home, but you're not leaving until you've had dinner here with us.'

'No, really I——'

'Please stay, Jessica,' Olivia cut across Jessica's apologetic refusal to the invitation.

It would take someone far stronger than herself to refuse the plea in those grey eyes, Jessica realised, and she sighed inwardly as she smiled down at Olivia. 'Thank you, I would like that very much.'

There was an undercurrent of excitement to the conversation when they sat around the teak table in the dining-room that evening. Frances, with her dark eyes shining, was bubbling over like a happy fountain as she related the events of that afternoon to her father and Peter O'Brien. Bernard looked upon her with pride, and Peter with some amusement, while Vivien made no effort to hide the deep affection she felt for the child.

Jessica, however, felt vaguely troubled about Vivien. She had gone strangely silent during dinner, and on a few occasions Jessica had caught a look of acute unhappiness flitting across her face. It made her wonder about Vivien, and the reason why she had never had any children of her own.

It was after eight that evening when Jessica looked in on Olivia to say goodnight, and she found her lying awake with a tired but happy smile hovering about her soft mouth.

'Jessica . . .' she began, gesturing a little helplessly with one slender hand, 'I haven't thanked you yet.'

'You have nothing to thank me for,' Jessica replied firmly, lowering her voice to match Olivia's.

'Oh, yes, I have,' Olivia argued. 'I knew that the call I sent out for Bernard wouldn't reach him in time, and I was absolutely petrified until you walked in here this afternoon.'

'You're to take things easy for the next few days, and I'll come out every day to check on you as well as the baby,' Jessica changed the subject and, leaning over the cradle, she took a last quick look at the pink-skinned and slightly wrinkled little human lying there so quietly. 'What are you going to call him, by the way?'

'We haven't decided yet.'

'I have the perfect name for him,' Bernard announced, entering the room and walking across to his wife's side to take the hand she extended towards him.

'Have you, darling?' Olivia smiled up at him tenderly.

'I can't think of a better name than Logan, can you?'

'Oh, Bernard!' Olivia smiled a little dubiously, but Bernard's face wore a look of granite-hard determination.

'Logan was Olivia's maiden name,' he explained to Jessica.

'It sounds good to me, and it's a strong name for a boy,' Jessica agreed, touching the tiny fingers lightly with her own. 'Goodnight, Logan. I'll see you and your mother tomorrow.'

'I'll walk you out to your car, Jessica,' Peter offered when he met her coming out of Olivia's room, and she smiled her thanks, realising that he wanted to have a private word with her concerning Olivia's confinement.

'Did everything go off all right?' Peter asked when they reached her Alfa. 'No complications?'

'None at all,' Jessica assured him.

'Good,' Peter nodded, his fair hair almost silver in the moonlight. 'Olivia's not a big woman, and I must admit that I was a little worried about her giving normal birth, but——' he shrugged selfconsciously, and smiled. 'When it's family you're dealing with, you're inclined to be more aware of all the dangers involved, and it's a damnable thing.'

'Vivien was a great help, and so was Frances,' Jessica told him, 'and you might thank them for me once again.'

'I'll do that,' he nodded, seeing her safely into her car.

It was after nine when Jessica finally arrived at the

cottage, and she was on the point of taking a refreshing bath when the telephone rang in the lounge.

'I've been trying to reach you all evening,' Dane Trafford's accusing voice came clearly over the line and, despite herself, her heart skipped a beat.

'I've been out at Mountain View,' she explained. 'Olivia King gave birth to a son late this afternoon.'

'You mean the baby was born out on the farm?'

'That's correct.'

Her affirmative answer caused an explosion to erupt at the other end of the line. 'Why the hell didn't she come in to the hospital?'

'There was no way she could get to the hospital, with her husband out in the bush hunting down an injured kudu.'

'You could have arranged for an ambulance to go out and collect her.'

'There wasn't time,' Jessica argued, becoming more than just annoyed.

'What do you mean, there wasn't time?' Dane demanded fiercely, and Jessica sighed inwardly.

'Olivia was already in the final stages of labour when I arrived out at Mountain View.'

'So what!' Dane replied cuttingly. 'Do you know how many women have hardly had time to cool their heels in hospital before their babies were born?'

'Hundreds, I suppose, but——'

'Then why the hell didn't you see to it that you brought her in to the hospital?'

'Because, Dr Trafford,' Jessica began, trying desperately to control her anger, 'I considered that my patient would prefer the comfort of her own bed to the back of a bumpy ambulance when it came to selecting a place for her baby to be born.'

'Oh, that's nice,' his cynical voice slided through her. 'You carry an emergency theatre around with you, no doubt, in case you should require it.'

'There's no need for you to be sarcastic!'

'I am not being sarcastic, damn you!' Dane exploded.

'Then what, in the name of heaven, are you trying to prove?' Jessica demanded, no longer troubling to keep her temper in check. 'Do you consider me incapable of dealing with emergencies?'

'How should I know whether you're capable or not?' he replied bitingly, denting her pride.

'Well, until you do, I suggest you keep your opinions to yourself, Dr Trafford,' she retorted icily, determined not to let him know how much his lack of confidence in her had hurt.

'Confound it, Jessica,' he sighed irritably, 'all I'm trying to say is that things wouldn't have looked so good if you had encountered complications with none of the necessary equipment to deal with it.'

He had a point, of course, she admitted to herself, but had he been there to examine Olivia as she had done, he would have seen for himself that the inconvenience of an ambulance journey would have been unnecessary.

'I did what I considered best for Olivia, and what I knew she would have preferred,' she said at last.

'One should expect that kind of reasoning from a woman, I suppose.'

'And what's that supposed to mean?' she demanded coldly.

'It's a known fact that women allow their judgment to be clouded by emotion, and you're a typical example of that,' he stated harshly.

'Emotion had nothing to do with my decision, Dr Trafford.'

'Didn't it?'

Jessica's knuckles whitened on the receiver with the effort to control the wave of fury that washed over her.

'Was there anything else, Dr Trafford?' she enquired

with a politeness that stuck in her throat.

'Yes,' he snapped, 'but it'll keep.'

The line went dead, and Jessica slammed the receiver back on to its cradle to find that she was shaking in every limb with the force of her anger.

'Damn the man!' she thought, her eyes dark and stormy. If he was not trying to seduce her, then he was treating her like a first-year medical student, and she could not decide at that moment which was worse. He was, at times, infuriating and insufferable, and this was one of those times.

Jessica slept very little that night. She was called out to the hospital in the early hours of the morning, and it was almost dawn before she arrived back at the cottage. She showered and changed, and watched the sun come up before making herself a slice of toast and coffee, but Sister Hansen was quick to notice the signs of weariness which Jessica had tried to hide with the aid of her make-up.

'You've had a busy night, it seems,' she remarked shrewdly when Jessica entered the consulting-rooms through the private entrance at the side of the building, 'And I can't promise you a quiet morning either. Dr O'Brien is at the hospital, and Dr Trafford has gone out to the clinic at the forestry department, so that more or less leaves you holding the fort, and the waiting-room is crowded with patients this morning.'

Jessica shrugged herself wearily into her white jacket and forced herself to smile. 'Then you'd better send the first patient in, Sister Hansen.'

That was the start of a morning the like of which Jessica had never experienced before. The steady stream of patients seemed endless, and added to that a truck-load of patients arrived from the neighbouring state of Venda. Jessica stared at the sea of black faces eyeing her with curiosity and interest, and she knew at last what one of her university professors had meant when he had said that there were times when one cursed the fact that you possessed only one pair of hands.

This was one of those occasions, Jessica groaned inwardly, and she set to work with grim determination while Sister Hansen tirelessly ushered the patients in and out of her rooms.

When Emily Hansen finally looked in on Jessica after the last patient had departed, she found a tired young woman sitting slumped in her chair with her eyes closed.

'It's been a rotten morning for you, Dr Neal, but can you imagine what it was like before you came?'

Jessica opened her eyes and smiled up at the woman who was clucking around her sympathetically. 'Do you know something, Sister Hansen? I admit that I'm tired, but I also admit to a tremendous satisfaction within myself. This is the kind of doctoring I've always wanted to do. The kind that leaves you bone weary, but satisfied.' Amusement lifted the corners of her mouth, and put a sparkle back in her eyes. 'If my father could have seen me this morning he would have been horrified!'

'Didn't your father like the idea of you becoming a doctor?'

'Oh, he liked the idea all right,' Jessica laughed, 'but he had something totally different in mind for me.'

Sister Hansen did not pretend that she understood, and neither did Jessica explain as she took off her white jacket and picked up her bag. 'I think I'll skip lunch and take a drive out to Mountain View to see Olivia and the baby. After that I'll be at the hospital if anyone needs me.'

Emily Hansen stared after her slim, retreating figure, and shook her head reprovingly. Doctors were always making their patients aware of the dangers of skipping meals, but they seldom took their own advice.

Jessica drove out to Mountain View at a leisurely pace. There was plenty of time before she had to be at the hospital that afternoon, and, besides that, she had a problem that she had been wrestling with ever since Vivien had relaxed her guard a fraction the day before. A plan was taking shape in her mind, but before she did anything about it she thought it advisable to find out a little more about Peter O'Brien's wife, and the one who could enlighten her was Olivia King.

A little sigh escaped Jessica, but it was lost above the sound of the Alfa's engine. Instead of the shimmering road ahead of her, she saw the lost expression on the face of a small, fair-haired little girl, and it brought a lump to her throat which was difficult to get rid of.

'Women allow emotion to cloud their judgment,' Dane Trafford's scathing remark leapt into her mind, and with an angry exclamation she thrust aside his disturbing and infuriating image to concentrate on her driving once more.

CHAPTER FIVE

As luck would have it, Jessica found Olivia alone out at Mountain View; alone, that was, except for the faithful Evalina and the rest of the servants. When Jessica had examined Olivia as well as the baby, she allowed herself to be persuaded to stay for a cup of tea and a slice of Evalina's delicious apple pie.

Jessica enjoyed talking to Olivia. She was an intelligent, well-read woman, and she gave no indication now of the insecurity she might once have experienced in her life.

'Vivien was here early this morning to bath little Logan,' Olivia said eventually, and her laughter fell softly on Jessica's ears. 'She just about had a fit when she heard that Evalina intended bathing him.'

This was the opening Jessica had been waiting for and, with a casualness which could not be faulted, she said: 'Vivien is fond of children, it seems.'

Olivia smiled and nodded. 'She adores Frances, and there's already a clear indication that Logan's aunt is going to spoil him abominably.'

'Why didn't she have any children of her own?'

Olivia's expression sobered. 'That's a subject Vivien never discusses, but Bernard told me that she was treated by several specialists before she was forced to accept the fact that she would never have children.'

'Did they never think of adopting a baby?'

'That I can't tell you, but Vivien has always given me the impression of someone who accepted the inevitable, and got on with the job of living.'

'You say that as though you don't quite believe it,' Jessica remarked daringly.

'I don't,' Olivia confessed. 'I think that, deep down, Vivien has wanted a child desperately, but the Kings are a proud family, and rather than admit defeat by adopting a baby, she decided to face up to the fact that she would never have a child by pretending that it didn't matter.'

'I see,' Jessica murmured, taking time off to digest the enormity of Olivia's personal observations.

'What's on your mind, Jessica?'

Jessica looked up quickly into those calm, smiling eyes. 'I have an idea, and if it works . . .'

'You'd better tell me about it,' Olivia suggested when Jessica left her sentence hanging tantalisingly in the air.

Jessica placed her empty tea cup in the tray on the bedside table, and plunged into what she had to say. 'There's a very unhappy ten-year-old little girl in the orphanage in Johannesburg. She survived an accident which robbed her of both her parents, and I became acquainted with her while she was still a patient in the hospital.' Jessica paused for breath and, glancing quickly at Olivia, she added: 'She has no one else, and I promised her I would arrange for her to spend one of her school holidays here with me.'

'I think I'm beginning to see what you're aiming at,' Olivia murmured thoughtfully. 'If Vivien takes this child to her heart, then she might consider giving her a home.'

Jessica nodded. 'Megan Leigh is a lovely child, and I can't see anyone not becoming fond of her. She loves easily, and she needs to be loved in return.'

'You know what, Jessica?' Olivia smiled eagerly. 'I hope with all my heart that it works.'

'Do you think I should go ahead and arrange for Megan to come and spend the September holidays here with me?'

'Why not?' Olivia demanded with a degree of excitement in her voice that matched Jessica's. 'The sooner we get this experiment under way, the sooner we'll know the results.'

Jessica flashed Olivia a grateful smile. 'I'm glad now that I thought to discuss this matter with you, Olivia.'

'I'm glad you did, and I shan't breathe a word to anyone,' Olivia promised. 'You realise, of course, that if Vivien should suspect anything, then the whole experiment might fail miserably.'

Jessica was only too aware of this, but when she finally drove back to town she was in a much lighter frame of mind. She would make the necessary arrangements as soon as possible, and it would at least give the child something to look forward to.

It was not until two days later that Jessica had the opportunity to make the necessary telephone call which would allow Megan to spend the spring holidays with her in Louisville, and when she finally replaced the receiver on its cradle there was a smile of intense satisfaction hovering about her mouth. All that remained now was for her to give her father a ring to ask him to collect the child at the end of that school term, and to see to it that she was put safely on a train bound for Louisville.

'Now what, I wonder, has brought on that smile of satisfaction,' a mocking voice remarked, and Jessica swung round in her chair to see Dane Trafford entering her consulting-room. 'Am I going to be enlightened, or must it remain a mystery for ever?' he demanded when she continued to sit there staring up at his lean, muscular frame which never failed to stir her senses in the most peculiar way.

'I've arranged for a little girl to spend the September holidays with me. She was orphaned at the beginning of this year,' she explained.

'Was she a patient of yours?'

'Indirectly, yes.'

Cynicism curved his mouth. 'That proves my point, doesn't it, that women doctors become too emotionally involved with their patients.'

Jessica pushed back her chair agitatedly, and rose to her feet, but she took great care to put a considerable distance between herself and the man who had seated himself on the corner of her desk before she said: 'I not only care about the state their bodies are in, I also happen to care about the mental state of my patients, and I'm not ashamed to admit it.'

'Spoken like a woman,' he mocked her.

'I should hope so,' she retaliated swiftly, 'because that's what I am.'

It was a mistake saying that, but she realised it too late, for his eyes were already travelling over her with that slow sensuality that nearly always succeeded in making her feel as if she had been stripped to the skin.

'I've been aware of that fact for quite some time,' he informed her with a derisive smile, and then he was gone before she could think of anything to say.

He was really the most abominable man, she decided furiously, her hands shaking while she packed her bag, then she said goodnight to Sister Hansen, and drove herself home.

A telephone call to her father that evening set her mind at rest. They would see to it that Megan Leigh was collected at the orphanage, and put on the first available train to Louisville at the end of that term.

'We're coming up to Louisville this weekend, then we can discuss the matter in more detail,' Jonathan Neal told his daughter. 'We should arrive there Friday afternoon, and we'll leave again on the Monday morning.'

'That's wonderful!'

'Will there be place for us to stay?'

'The cottage has a guest room.'

'Fine,' Jonathan sighed. 'That should put your mother's mind at rest. You know how she hates hotels.'

'Give her my love, and tell her not to worry,' Jessica laughed.

'She's not the only one who happens to be worried, and that's why we're coming up there to see you.' There was a pause as if he expected her to say something, but when she remained silent he merely sighed once more and said: 'Oh, well, we'll have a long chat when we're there.'

They said goodbye shortly afterwards, but her conversation with her father had left Jessica feeling faintly amused. They would, no doubt, find it difficult to accept that she was happy in what she was doing, but it would be up to her to convince them.

She took a quick shower and exchanged her neat, serviceable skirt and blouse for an apricot-coloured silk dress which was cool against her skin. She was looking forward to a quiet evening at home; the first in a long time. She would make herself something to eat, and afterwards she would catch up on the latest information in the medical journal which came in the post.

It was a delightful thought, but no sooner had she taken a piece of steak out of the refrigerator when Dane Trafford burst into her cottage, almost wrenching the front door from its hinges.

'Drop whatever you're doing, and come with me,' he ordered, looking unfamiliar in a white, open-necked sports shirt, and grey denim pants. 'It's an emergency.'

Jessica thrust the steak back into the refrigerator without hesitation. 'I'll get my bag.'

'Leave it!' he rapped out the command. 'I have everything we'll need.'

Jessica obeyed without question, stopping only to lock the cottage door behind her, but when she sat beside him in his Mustang she could contain her curiosity no longer.

'What is it?' she asked anxiously. 'What's happened?'

'It's not what has happened. It's what's still *going* to happen.'

'What do you mean, it's what's still going to happen?'

she questioned frowningly, her frantic mind skirting over the frightening possibility of an anticipated disaster.

'Shut up, will you, and let me concentrate on my driving,' Dane ordered tersely, and Jessica lapsed obediently into silence.

Dane was driving as fast as the speed limit would allow, and just beyond the limits of the town he turned off on to a side road which led up to an old house which stood on an enormous piece of ground. It was difficult to make out her surroundings in the dark, but she was almost certain that she had glimpsed a tennis court and swimming pool to the right of the house. The house itself had obviously had its outward appearance altered quite recently, and the lights shining out on to the patio gave no indication of an impending disaster.

'Come with me,' Dane said when she had climbed out of the car and, taking her arm, he hurried her up the stone steps towards the heavy oak door. He opened it without knocking, and moments later Jessica found herself in a spacious entrance hall with the chandelier from the ceiling casting a patterned light on to the polished yellow-wood floor. 'Welcome to my home, Jessica.'

She stared up at him blankly for several incredulous seconds before her mind was able to absorb and digest his statement, then an incredible anger began to shake through her.

'This is your home?' she asked coldly, making sure that she had heard him correctly as she watched him calmly pocket his car keys.

'That's right,' he nodded.

'And where, may I ask, is the emergency?' she demanded, her voice rife with sarcasm.

'You're looking at it,' he told her mockingly. 'I just couldn't face dining alone this evening.'

Her dark eyes, sparkling with fury, traced the hard, arrogant line of his square jaw, and that husky note in her voice was intensified as she unleashed some of the anger within her. 'You tricked me into coming here!'

'Would you have come if I'd invited you?'

'Most certainly not!'

'Well, there you are, then.'

Her hands were shaking with the desire to strike him, and she was forced to clench them tightly at her sides. 'You're mad!'

'I dare say I am,' he laughed shortly.

'Take me home this instant!'

'I'll take you home after you've had dinner with me.'

'In that case I'll walk home.'

He was at the door before she could reach it, applying his weight to the solid oak, and imprisoning her there at the same time.

'It's a mighty long walk back to your cottage,' he cautioned her, 'and it's dangerous for a woman to thumb a lift at this time of night.'

'I don't care!' Jessica argued fiercely, fighting desperately against the emotions aroused by the closeness of his hard, virile body. 'You had no right to bring me here under false pretences, and if you don't want to take me home, then I'll just have to——'

'Jessica,' he interrupted her tirade sharply, 'are you afraid of me?'

She looked away from those razor-sharp eyes. 'Don't be ridiculous!'

'Then stay and have dinner with me.'

The clean male smell of him invaded her nostrils and stirred her senses alarmingly, but she refused to be swayed in a physical sense. 'I claim the right to choose whom I spend my free time with, and I don't choose to spend it with you.'

'That's not a very nice thing to say, Jessica.'

'I'm not in a very nice mood at this moment.'

'All you have to do is have dinner with me, and at any

time during the course of the evening you have only to say the word, and I'll take you home.' Her chin was caught between strong fingers, and her face was raised in a way that left her no option but to meet the challenging mockery of those pale grey eyes. 'Am I asking for something so impossible?'

She had never been this close to him before, and her heart was beating too hard and fast for comfort, but, *damn him*, she would rather die than have him know of the shattering effect his nearness was having on her emotions.

'If you refuse to take me home now, then I don't suppose I have much of a choice, do I?' she heard herself reply in a surprisingly calm voice.

'Come this way,' he said, releasing her and, at the same time, giving her the opportunity to breathe easier as he led the way into the living-room. Jessica paused just inside the door, her eyes widening at what she saw. 'Do you like it?' Dane asked with a faint smile playing about his mouth.

'Not particularly,' she said, taking in the subdued lighting, the expensive hi-fi, the shaggy carpet, and the heavily padded furniture.

'If it's the truth I want, then I'm sure to get it from you, Jessica,' he laughed cynically, drawing her farther into the room. 'What is there that you don't like?'

'The whole set-up,' she told him stiffly, casting a wary glance about the room once more. 'It looks like a seduction scene in a third-rate movie.'

He gave a shout of laughter. 'Now what would a nice girl like you know about things like that?'

'I'm not a child!'

'No, you're not.' His glance lingered briefly on her slight, feminine curves, then he turned away with a careless shrug. 'It's a pity you don't like the way I've furnished this room, because I find it rather relaxing. Soft lights, sweet music . . .' he flicked a switch and the sound of muted violins reached her ears, '. . . and comfortable chairs in which to enjoy it all.'

'Chairs? What chairs?' Jessica pounced on the word nervously. 'There are two sofas, and neither of them look as if they were designed for the purpose of being sat on.'

'Don't put ideas into my head, Jessica.'

'I don't have to put them there. They're there all the time,' she retorted with heavy sarcasm, but, against her will, a strange excitement was beginning to stir within her when her eyes collided with his. 'Did you bring me here to seduce me?'

'If I said no, would you believe me?'

'I most certainly would not!'

'Then you're a wise girl,' he smiled wickedly, turning towards the glass cabinet at the far end of the room.

'You admit it, then?' she almost choked on the words.

'Let's say that I intend to be on my best behaviour, and the rest is entirely up to you.'

'You mean you'll at least give me the opportunity to say no?' she asked with a marked cynicism in her voice.

Dane splashed soda water into his drink and filled a smaller glass with something she could not identify before he turned and said: 'Difficult as it may be for you to believe, Jessica, I've never yet taken a woman by force.'

'Am I supposed to find some sort of comfort in that remark?'

He appeared unconcerned as he came towards her with those lithe, easy strides, but she sensed that every muscle in his long, lean body was geared for action at a moment's notice.

'My revealing remark was intended to help you relax,' he replied, and her winged eyebrows rose higher above her mocking eyes.

'Oh, really?'

'I have no intention of pouncing on you, and neither do I have the inclination to drag you by the hair into my bed,' he announced derisively, a look of exasperation flashing across his handsome features. 'Nothing would dampen my ardour more.'

'Well, that's nice to know at any rate,' she replied stiffly.

'Here,' he said abruptly, almost thrusting the small glass into her hand, 'drink this.'

Jessica stared down into the crimson liquid a little dubiously. 'What is it?'

'It's a love potion I blended myself,' he informed her harshly. 'It's guaranteed to make you break out in a feverish and passionate desire for . . .' he bowed mockingly '. . . yours truly.'

'Don't be silly,' she laughed, but her laughter was unsteady.

'You're the one who's being silly,' he contradicted. 'I've given you a harmless glass of wine which is about as potent as tapwater.'

Jessica felt more than silly; she felt ridiculous as she allowed herself to be coaxed on to the sofa where the soft cushions seemed to enfold her like a cloud. Dane was seated beside her, and his eyes never left her in peace for one moment. There was seduction in every look and in every nuance of his voice, and she was alarmed to discover that she was responding to it much the same as the dove outside her bedroom window responded to the call of its mate. She was becoming hypnotised by his suave charm, and she had to escape before it was too late.

'This is impossible!' she muttered angrily, rising to her feet and placing her untouched glass of wine on the low table. 'I can't stay.'

'Of course you can,' Dane contradicted, placing his own glass beside hers, and getting to his feet to put her at a disadvantage once more. 'Peter is on call, and that means we have the entire evening to ourselves.'

'That's just it,' she argued nervously. 'I can't spend the evening here with you.'

His eyes narrowed perceptibly. 'Are you afraid of what people might say?'

'Don't pretend that you're unaware of the reputation you've acquired for yourself.'

'I have no intention of pretending anything, but may I remind you that you came here in my car. No one saw me arrive, and no one saw us leave so, to all intents and purposes, you are safely tucked up in your cottage.'

'I would still prefer to go home,' she persisted stubbornly, but she should have known that she would be no match for this man who towered above her with his jaw hard and unrelenting.

His hands came up to grip her shoulders, his touch burning her skin and sending a quivering warmth flowing through her body. The edge of the sofa was against her calves, and a gentle push sent her down into its cloudy softness once more.

'Drink your wine, and relax,' Dane instructed, pressing her glass into her trembling hand and seating himself so closely beside her that his hard thigh brushed against her own. 'The evening has only just begun.'

'Dr Trafford——'

'Dane,' he murmured, sliding an arm along the back of the sofa behind her shoulders, and his particular brand of shaving cream tantalised her senses. 'For tonight it must be Dane.'

Jessica stared helplessly into those cool grey eyes. 'You don't give up easily, do you, Dane?'

'Not when I think I have something worthwhile in my sights,' he replied smoothly, reaching for his own glass and draining it before he returned it to the low table.

'Meaning me?' she asked, holding her breath.

'Meaning you.'

She wrenched her glance from his and, taking a sip of the wine to steady the trembling of her insides, she said bluntly, 'I'm not available for what you have in mind.'

'How do you know what I have in mind?' he demanded mockingly, his sensual fingers trailing fire against her sensitive skin at the nape of her neck.

'I've been in Louisville just over a month, and judging by what I've heard and seen for myself, I can guess.'

'You're referring to Sylvia Summers, I take it?'

'You take it correctly, but——' she altered her position to avoid his touch, 'your private life is your own, just as long as you don't insist on dragging me into it as well.'

Dane leaned towards her then, imprisoning her in the curved corner of the sofa, and making her aware once again of the potent magnetism he exuded. His hard thigh pressed against her own with a certain intimacy, and it sent a shiver of sensation rippling through her.

'You don't seem to have a very flattering opinion of me,' he remarked mockingly, his lips so close to her own that she could feel the warmth of his breath against her mouth when he spoke, and for one despicable moment she wondered what it would feel like to have those sensually chiselled lips pressed against her own.

Taking care not to spill her wine, she said accusingly, 'I don't particularly care for men who use women merely to satisfy their sexual appetites.'

His mouth twisted cynically. 'Women like Sylvia don't expect or want more than that from a man.'

'I dare say you're right, but even women like Sylvia need the stability of marriage at some time or another in their lives,' she stopped him in the act of bringing his lips closer to hers, and he drew away from her with an exclamation of disgust on his lips.

'Marriage!' he sneered harshly. 'What can marriage offer me that I don't already have?'

'A family,' she said at once and, taking another steadying sip of wine, she asked, 'Don't you want children, Dane?'

'To have children I shall have to find myself a wife first, and I can't say that I relish the idea of tying myself down to one woman for the rest of my life.' For some unaccountable reason she felt a painful jar in the region of her heart, and, as she raised her glass to her lips, he said with an exasperated sigh, 'Now how did we get on to this subject, may I know?'

'I'm not so sure,' Jessica replied tritely, 'but perhaps it would be safer if we stepped off it.'

Dane leaned towards her with a look of purposeful intent on his lean, tanned face, but a discreet knock on the living-room door made them both glance towards it to find a black man in a neat white jacket hovering there.

'Dinner is ready, Mr. Dane.'

Dane sighed audibly, and drew away from Jessica. 'Thank you, Jonas.'

A superbly prepared four-course meal was served to them in the large dining-room with Jonas coming and going discreetly. He was accustomed to his employer entertaining women alone in his home, it seemed, and she experienced the most hateful pang of jealousy when she found herself wondering at the number of women who had sat exactly where she was sitting as a prelude to an evening which had undoubtedly ended in his bed.

Jessica thrust aside this distasteful thought and tried to concentrate on the plate of food before her, but she found it virtually impossible to continue enjoying the tastefully prepared beef and freshly cooked vegetables.

'You're an excellent surgeon, Dane,' she directed the conversation along a safer passage when they sat with their coffee before them. 'Have you ever thought of specialising in the various fields of surgery?'

'Neuro-surgery interests me a great deal,' Dane's reply surprised her, 'and if I should ever grow tired of my job here in Louisville, I might just take the plunge in that direction.'

'In that case you should chat to my father,' she was saying before she could prevent herself, and his straight, dark brows drew together in a frown.

'Your father?'

Jessica lowered her gaze uncomfortably. 'My father specialised in neuro-surgery, but he retired last year.'

'Why didn't you mention this before?'

'I didn't think it was important,' she moved her shoulders carelessly, wishing for some obscure reason that she had not mentioned the subject.

'Am I going to have the privilege of meeting your father?'

'You may, yes,' she replied evasively and, risking a glance at him, she found him observing her with an unfathomable expression in his grey eyes.

'I shall have something to look forward to, then.'

When they returned to the living-room Dane selected a record from his vast collection and put it on the turntable, then he turned towards her and held out his hand.

'Dance with me, Jessica,' he said, his eyes holding hers captive, and she felt powerless to resist as he drew her up out of the sofa and into his arms.

Jessica had danced with many men before, but dancing with Dane was a totally new experience. His hand was against the hollow of her back, drawing her strangely pliant body against the hard length of his, and sparking off all kinds of sensations. His thighs brushed against hers as they moved slowly in time to the rhythmic, throbbing beat of the music, and when he laid her hand against his chest where she could feel the warmth of his skin through his shirt, she was surprised to discover that his heart was beating as hard and fast as her own. His potent maleness made the blood flow through her veins like heady wine, and when he lowered his head to rest his cheek against hers, she found that she had neither the strength nor the desire to bring this moment to an end.

She could not be sure how long they danced like that. The music seemed endless, but somehow she did not care. She had the mad desire to stay in his arms like this for ever, with his cheek against hers, and the warmth of his hard flesh burning her fingers through the expensive cotton of his shirt, but she knew it could not last when she felt Dane's hand move in a sensually arousing manner against the hollow of her back, and she stirred against him even though her capricious body was beginning to yearn for something more.

'I'm finding it extremely difficult being on my best behaviour with you,' he smiled down at her twistedly, and his voice deepened on a note of passion which was beginning to find an echo within her.

'Perhaps it's time you took me home,' she managed huskily, drawing a little away from him as she felt him tense.

'You're not serious.'

'I'm afraid I am,' she smiled a little shakily, not trusting herself to say more at that moment.

'Well,' he sighed resignedly, releasing her with the light of mockery back in his eyes, 'I did say that I would take you home at any time during the course of the evening, didn't I?'

An impregnable silence seemed to settle between them during the drive back to her cottage. Was he angry? she wondered. Or couldn't he care less? There were, she supposed miserably, plenty of women only too willing to give him what she had refused.

'I'm not going to invite you in, Dane,' she said, unlocking the door of the cottage, but his hand reached over her shoulder and pushed the door open further.

'I'm coming in all the same,' he announced, following her inside and, taking the keys from the lock, he closed the door behind him.

'This has gone far enough!' Jessica exclaimed, nervous and seeking refuge in anger as she flicked on the lights in the lounge.

'I agree with you,' Dane said tersely, dropping her keys on to the low table, and grasping her firmly by the shoulders. 'Dammit, Jessica, you're the most frustrating woman I've ever met!'

The look in his eyes sparked off a danger signal in her mind, but she chose to ignore it as she shrugged herself free, and marched away from him towards the kitchen. 'I'll make you a cup of coffee, and then you're going home.'

The coffee was never made. When she switched on the kettle he reached from behind her to switch it off again and, pivoting to face him, the angry burst of words died instantly on her lips. She was wedged between Dane and the steel cupboard, and danger lurked in those narrowed, glittering eyes. She was short, and he was tall. *Too* damned tall, she decided as he towered above her menacingly with his wide shoulders blotting out the light which hung from the kitchen ceiling, and she knew suddenly that indescribable fear of an animal trapped with no escape hatch in sight.

His hands were spanning her slim waist, his fingers biting through the silk of her dress into the flesh below her ribcage and, before she could begin to suspect what he had in mind, she found herself lifted off the floor until her wide, startled eyes were on a level with his.

'Put me down at once!' she ordered sharply, her hands clutching instinctively at his shoulders where the bulging muscles rippled beneath her touch, but the look in those eyes so close to her own told her that he had no intention of doing as she had requested.

'Put your arms around my neck and kiss me.'

His words fell like pebbles on the already disturbed surface of her mind, and her eyes darkened with anger and alarm. She felt like kicking his shins, but she knew without being told that she would regret such an action.

'I'll do nothing of the kind!' she exclaimed at last in a choked voice, and her futile efforts to escape merely evoked his mocking laughter.

'You weigh hardly anything at all, Jessica, and I'm quite prepared to stand here like this until you do as I say.'

And he would too, she realised frantically, loving yet hating the feel of his hard body against her own at that moment.

'You're detestable, Dane Trafford!' she hissed fiercely.

'And you're adorable when you're angry,' he grinned. 'Kiss me.'

He was immovable on this subject and, putting her arms hesitantly around his neck as he had instructed, she brushed her lips briefly against his.

'Do you call that a kiss?' he laughed harshly.

'Yes,' she snapped, her face suffused with abominable colour. 'Now let me go at once!'

'Not until you've kissed me properly,' he instructed in an undaunted manner. 'Put your lips against mine, and this time count to ten before you take them away.'

Jessica was becoming desperate, and if this was the only way she was going to get rid of him, then she would simply have to indulge him in his foolishness. She lowered her lids over eyes that sparkled with fury, and pressed her lips against his.

One . . . two . . . three . . . four . . .! It was not fair, but something was happening which she had not bargained for. His mouth had opened over hers, and her own lips had parted, allowing him to invade her mouth with a sensual intimacy that sent exciting little tremors cavorting across receptive nerves. She could have drawn her lips from his at any time, but she didn't, and the kiss went on . . . and on . . . until every scrap of resistance died within her to leave her pliant and responsive.

It was Dane who drew back a fraction to murmur against her lips, 'That was quite something, wasn't it?'

The hint of mockery in his voice should have angered her, but instead her fingers tightened in his dark hair, and this was enough encouragement for him to seek her lips again. She had kissed before, but never like this, and never before had a man's kisses awakened such a tumult of emotions within her.

Dane released her unexpectedly, setting her on her feet with a muttered curse on his lips. She blinked up into those pale, glittering eyes in a dazed, bewildered fashion, but before she could come to her senses she found herself draped across one hard arm, and her head was being forced back by the pressure of his mouth against her own. His passion, unleashed, was like the eruption of a violent storm and, caught in the midst of it, she could only cling to him while the devastation swept over her. Impatient fingers tugged at the zip of her dress, and the catch of her bra was no obstacle in his path. Somewhere from the drugged recesses of her mind came the warning to resist, but the sensual pressure of those clever fingers against her taut breast was igniting delicious little fires in her body which were spreading and gathering momentum until she knew the sweet agony of desire. She would despise herself later, but not now; not this minute.

'I want you, Jessica,' Dane groaned against her quivering mouth, and his words acted like a douche of iced water on her fiery emotions, making her draw away from him to hold him at arm's length.

'Just like that?' she asked, lowering her dark lashes to hide the shame and the pain that mingled in her eyes.

'Just like that,' he confirmed abruptly, and a little callously, she thought.

'I'm sorry, Dane,' she said, escaping from his arms and pushing past him on legs that felt peculiarly like jelly. 'I'm not in the market for that kind of relationship.'

'I'd make sure you don't regret it.'

'I don't doubt that your experience as a lover would see to that,' she laughed bitterly, her body still tingling with the expertise of his caresses as she turned to face him from a safe distance. 'I'm still a bit old-fashioned about such things, I'm afraid. I don't believe in sleeping around.'

'I detest that phrase "sleeping around",' he told her with a look of distaste flashing across his lean face. 'I'm not asking you to sleep around, but merely to let me make love to you.'

'That's just it, Dane,' she remarked coldly after having won her battle to regain at least part of her composure. 'Love wouldn't enter into it at all; only lust, and I would end up feeling disgusted with myself.'

His eyes mirrored mocking disbelief as they played over her small, slim figure standing so erect in the middle of the neat kitchen. 'How can you be sure?'

'I know myself, Dane, and it wouldn't work.'

Her hands fumbled awkwardly with the zip of her dress, and he came towards her, reaching behind her to pull it up deftly. Embarrassment stained her cheeks pink, but when she would have stepped away from him, his hand moved with swift precision to clasp a handful of hair at the back of her head, forcing her to meet the derisive mockery in his eyes.

'What am I going to do about you, Jessica?'

'Strike me off your list of possible conquests, and stick to women like Sylvia Summers,' she said with her heart beating in her mouth, and a terrible emptiness settling in her breast.

'Perhaps that's exactly what I shall do,' he announced, wounding her more than he would ever know, and then his mouth clamped down on hers with a bruising intensity that left her pale and shaken when he finally released her. 'Goodnight, Jessica.'

CHAPTER SIX

JESSICA arrived home on the Friday afternoon to find Vivien entertaining her parents, and the invitation had been issued for the three of them to dine with the O'Briens that evening. Jonathan and Amelia were both enchanted with Vivien, whose charm and sophistication was undeniable, and when Peter finally arrived home Jessica barely managed to get a word in edgeways to her father.

As the evening progressed she realised that her parents were no longer in doubt about her decision to come to Louisville. Her father was enjoying a discussion with Peter on the latest medical data, and her mother was too busy admiring Vivien's delightful home.

When they finally retired to Jessica's cottage, both Jonathan and Amelia agreed that Louisville was not such a bad town after all, and they went to bed tired but contented after their long journey that day.

Peter very kindly took Jonathan on a tour of the hospital the following morning, leaving Jessica alone with her mother, who wanted to know more about whether her daughter was not working too hard, and whether she was having the proper meals.

'I'm fine, Mother. Don't worry about me,' Jessica laughed reassuringly and, to set her mother's mind at rest, she told her of the many times she had arrived home a little late to find that Vivien had left her a cooked meal in the oven.

'She's a wonderful woman,' Amelia admitted with a grateful smile.

'Everyone here has been very kind to me, and I enjoy my work very much.'

It was not until after lunch that afternoon that Jessica

had the opportunity to speak to her father alone. Her mother was resting in the guest room, and when Jessica had tidied the kitchen she joined her father in the lounge. Jonathan was full of praise for the new, modern hospital he had visited that morning, and they discussed his tour in detail.

'I must say, Jessica, that Peter O'Brien has impressed me a great deal,' Jonathan changed the subject eventually, stretching out his legs before him, and lying back in his chair with his pipe clenched between his teeth. 'What's his partner like?'

'Dane Trafford?' Jessica hoped that she did not look as startled as she felt at that moment. 'Oh, he's . . . he's a very good doctor, and an excellent surgeon. He also happens to be very interested in neuro-surgery.'

'Is that so?' Jonathan's dark eyes lit up with interest. 'Am I going to meet him?'

'I don't imagine so. I——' The look of disappointment which flashed across her father's face made her change her mind reluctantly. 'Shall I give him a ring and ask him to join us for tea this afternoon?'

'Why not?' her father smiled, sending a cloud of smoke up towards the ceiling, and filling the room with the aromatic odour of his tobacco.

The telephone was not in its usual place in the lounge. Jessica had left it plugged in beside her bed, but it was just as well that her father could not see her, for her fingers trembled as she looked up Dane's number and dialled it. It rang only briefly at the other end before it was answered, but the voice that came over the line was definitely not Dane's. It was a feminine, feline purr, and Jessica felt a cold, sick feeling lodge itself at the pit of her stomach.

'Is that Dr Trafford's home?' she heard herself ask unnecessarily.

'Yes, it is, but Dr Trafford is off duty this weekend, so may I suggest that you call his partner, Dr O'Brien.'

The line went dead abruptly, cutting across Jessica's murmured 'Thank you', and her eyes were dark pools of pain as she slowly returned the receiver to its cradle.

'Will he come?' Jonathan asked eagerly when Jessica returned to the lounge.

'I'm afraid not.' She sat down heavily on the arm of the chair which she had vacated prior to making that call to Dane's home. 'He . . . he has another engagement.'

'Pity,' Jonathan frowned with disappointment, then his dark glance sharpened. 'You've gone rather pale, Jessica. Is something wrong?'

'Mild indigestion,' she prevaricated with a forced smile. 'I'll switch on the kettle and make us a pot of tea. Mother should be awake soon.'

'You fool!' she cursed herself silently when she was alone in the kitchen. 'You knew from the start what kind of man Dane Trafford was, and yet you allowed yourself to——'

She jerked her thoughts to an abrupt halt. She had allowed herself to what? Fall in love with him? Impossible! He was not at all the kind of man she could fall in love with, and yet . . . why did it hurt so much to think of him with another woman in his arms?

'It's not hurt you're feeling, Jessica Neal,' she told herself fiercely, 'it's disgust!'

Disgust! She clung to the word with a desperate urgency, but the pain did not ease, and neither did she dare allow herself further time to analyse what she was feeling.

The weekend was over much too soon, and it was perhaps a blessing that Jessica did not see Dane until late on Monday afternoon. She had called Peter in to discuss one of her patients with him, and the conversation had inevitably turned to her parents when Dane walked in, looking immaculate as always in white pants and matching safari jacket, the colour accentuating his tanned fitness.

'What a pity you didn't meet Jessica's parents over the weekend, Dane,' Peter remarked pleasantly, preparing to leave. 'Jessica's father, Jonathan Neal, is really one of the most interesting medical men I've spoken to yet, and you would have found his knowledge on neuro-surgery most enlightening.'

Dane did not reply, but his mouth tightened and, when the door closed behind Peter's lean frame, he asked coldly, 'Why didn't you let me know that your parents were spending the weekend with you?'

Jessica slid off the corner of her desk and, afraid that he would see the ridiculous trembling of her hands, she thrust them into the pockets of her white jacket, and crossed the room to stand staring out of the window with unseeing eyes.

'I did telephone your home Saturday afternoon with an invitation for you to join us for tea, but I discovered that you were fully occupied.'

'Ah, yes . . . Sylvia.' His voice sounded grim, but not at all apologetic as he joined her beside the window. 'I suppose she took the call?'

Jessica shrugged with a casualness she was far from experiencing. 'I presume it was her, unless you had more than one woman spending the weekend with you.'

The atmosphere was heavily charged, then a heavy hand came down on to her shoulder and she was turned round to face him. 'One word from you, Jessica, and Sylvia Summers will become part of my past.'

'And how long, I wonder, before you say the same about me to someone else?' she demanded cynically.

'Dammit, Jessica!' His hand left her shoulder as if she had stung him, and his narrowed eyes were like twin fires licking her upturned face. 'I've never wanted another woman as much as I want you.'

'I should feel flattered, I suppose, but I don't,' she heard herself projecting her voice beyond the tightness in her aching throat. 'If you want the truth, then I feel only degradation.'

'My God!' His face went strangely white beneath his

tan, and the hands that gripped her shoulders bit into them as if he wanted to crush the fragile bones beneath her jacket, but it was the cold fury in his eyes that frightened her most of all as he lashed her with his tongue. 'I'm willing to bet that degradation had nothing to do with what you felt the other night when I kissed you. What you felt was plain old-fashioned desire, so don't look down your pretty little nose at me, Jessica Neal, or I might decide to prove to you here and now what a damned liar you are!'

Stabs of numbing pain shot into her shoulders and down the length of her arms, but it was nothing compared to the renewed bout of pain she was experiencing in the region of her heart.

'You're hurting me,' she finally managed in a husky voice.

'Be thankful that my hands are not about your throat,' he bit out the words with a savagery that made her flinch inwardly, 'because I've never felt more like strangling anyone in my life!'

He released her then, and she staggered back against the windowsill, biting down hard on her quivering lip, and thankful that Dane did not see her agonised expression following him from her consulting-room. He closed the door behind him with a decisiveness that made her wince, and she suspected that he was shutting himself off from her with a finality that hurt more deeply than anything had done before.

Jessica's suspicions were correct. During the weeks that followed Dane treated her with the cool politeness of a stranger, and it was during those weeks that she discovered exactly how much she missed his mocking, often taunting remarks. However cynical his smile might have been, he had at least favoured her with it occasionally, but these days she encountered only the tight-lipped expression of her superior, and however much she disliked admitting it, he *was* her superior. She loved him. She could admit it to herself now, but it was too late, and neither did she want her love abused by a man who had no use for it.

Jessica was returning from a call-out to one of the farms in the district when she called in to see Olivia and the baby. She seldom drove past Mountain View these days without stopping for a cup of tea and a chat when she had the time, and today was one of those days when she felt the need to share her excitement with someone and that someone was Olivia King.

As always, they had tea out on the cool, gauzed-in verandah, and Logan slept contentedly in his pram while Jessica and Olivia talked quietly. Their conversation seldom ended these days without discussing the child who was coming on a visit to Louisville, but there was a gleam of eager anticipation in Olivia's grey eyes on this occasion as she asked,

'When are you expecting Megan?'

'She'll be arriving tomorrow on the early morning train,' Jessica replied, unable to hide her own eagerness.

'Have you told Vivien about her?'

'I mentioned only very briefly that Megan would be coming to stay for a while,' Jessica smiled conspiratorially. 'I asked if she would object to Megan playing in the garden during the day while I'm at the consulting-rooms.'

'What did she say?'

'You know Vivien,' Jessica laughed. 'She said she had no objection at all, and she went farther than that. She offered to see to it that Megan was fed and looked after when I couldn't manage to make it home for lunch.'

Olivia's expression sobered. 'Oh, I hope it works.'

'So do I,' Jessica echoed fervently. She was taking a gamble, and there was no guarantee at all that it would pay off.

Despite Olivia's backing, Jessica spent a restless night wondering yet again whether she had done the right thing. What if Megan and Vivien didn't take to each other?

What if they did, but Vivien failed to grasp the opportunity placed within her reach? What if . . .?

'Stop it!' she told herself sharply, rolling over on to her left side and thumping her pillow into shape with a clenched fist. 'It's an experiment, and if it doesn't work, then no one will have been hurt.'

It was with this thought in mind that she finally managed to fall asleep, but she was up again before dawn, and she was pacing the station platform when the sun rose like a red, fiery ball in the eastern sky.

'The train should be here any minute now, Dr Neal,' the stationmaster replied to Jessica's anxious query, and not two minutes later she saw the diesel engine coming round the bend further down the track.

A fair head bobbed out of a window as the train came to a squealing halt, and an arm was waving frantically. 'Dr Jessica!'

Jessica waved back, and moments later Megan was running towards her with a small suitcase clutched in her hand. She flung herself into Jessica's arms with a force that made Jessica stagger, but she managed somehow to maintain her balance, and tightened her arms about the child.

'It's good to see you again, Megan,' she laughed, dropping a light kiss on the child's honey-gold curls, and hugging her tightly.

'I missed you.'

'I missed you, too,' Jessica confessed, smiling down into wide blue eyes, then she gently ruffled the golden curls and picked up the suitcase that had been dumped carelessly at her feet. 'Come on, let's go. We can talk on the way, and I'm anxious for you to see where I live.'

Megan talked non-stop all the way to the cottage, telling Jessica about how Jonathan Neal had fetched her at the orphanage in his Mercedes, about the parcel of goodies Amelia had given her, and, most exciting of all, the train journey from Johannesburg. Jessica listened to it all without interrupting, and with a tender smile curving her soft mouth. She had never known Megan this animated before, but it was a welcome change from the woebegone little girl she had come to know at the beginning of that year.

When they arrived at the cottage Megan investigated every room while Jessica fried bacon and eggs for their breakfast. Megan's appetite was incredible. 'We never have bacon, and we don't always have eggs for breakfast in the orphanage,' she explained. 'Only on special occasions.'

Jessica did not query those special occasions, but merely pushed the dish of bacon closer to Megan's plate, and watched them disappear swiftly and hungrily.

They had barely washed the dishes when Jessica glanced out the window to see Vivien coming along the path towards the cottage, and there was a nervous flutter at the pit of her stomach when Vivien's voice called from the front door, 'May I come in?'

'Yes, of course, Vivien,' Jessica called back. 'We're in the kitchen.'

'I baked a batch of small cakes last night,' Vivien said, placing a cake tin on the kitchen table, but as she spoke her dark eyes travelled towards Megan, and remained there. 'I thought you might like to have a few with your tea some time.'

'That was kind of you, Vivien.' Jessica's heart was beating hard against her ribs and, placing an arm about Megan's small shoulders, she said: 'Megan, this is Mrs O'Brien. Her husband is also a doctor.'

'Hello, Mrs O'Brien,' Megan said shyly.

'I'm very glad to meet you, Megan, and please call me Aunty Vivien,' she said, taking the hand Megan had offered her and smiling warmly down into Megan's blue eyes. 'Mrs O'Brien is such a mouthful, don't you think?'

Megan agreed with shy reserve, then Vivien glanced at Jessica who had been observing this meeting with casual intent. 'You're on call this afternoon, aren't you, Jessica?'

'Yes, I'm afraid so,' Jessica sighed.

'I'm going out to Mountain View this afternoon,' Vivien announced. 'I could take Megan with me to meet Frances, and I'm sure she would enjoy the afternoon on the farm.'

'Do you have a farm, Aunty Vivien?' Megan wanted to know, her shyness forgotten in this moment of eager anticipation.

Vivien shook her head and smiled. 'It's my brother's farm, but he has a little girl called Frances who is about three years older than you, and I'm sure she would love to show you all the interesting things on her father's farm.' Vivien raised her hand and brushed it lightly over Megan's fair curls. 'Would you like to come with me?'

Blue eyes looked up into Jessica's questioningly. 'May I, Dr Jessica?'

'Of course you may, Megan.'

'I'll pick you up directly after lunch, then, Megan,' Vivien told the child and, glancing at Jessica, she said: 'See you later.'

Jessica expelled the air slowly and cautiously from her lungs, and the tension within her eased considerably.

'She's nice,' Megan observed as they watched Vivien take the path back to her house.

'Yes, she's very nice,' Jessica acknowledged, then she took Megan's hand and led her from the kitchen. 'Let's go and unpack your suitcase.'

Jessica opened the small suitcase and stared at the few nondescript items of clothing it contained. There was also a toothbrush, a towel, a comb and a brush for her hair, and that was practically the sum total of Megan's possessions.

'Hm . . .' Jessica frowned thoughtfully. 'I think that you and I ought to go out and do a bit of shopping. You could do with a few extra dresses as well as a couple of shorts and T-shirts to play about in.'

Megan's small face looked incredulous. 'Are you going to buy me new clothes?'

'Yes, I am.' Jessica's chin was set in a determined manner. 'Come on, let's lock up the cottage and start our raid on the shops.'

Jessica could not decide afterwards which of them had enjoyed the shopping spree more, Megan or herself, but when they emerged from the children's boutique an hour later, loaded with parcels, Megan announced excitedly, 'That was fun!'

'I think you have enough there now, don't you?' Jessica smiled down at her.

'Oh, yes!' Megan announced, her small face glowing with delight. 'Thank you, Dr Jessica.'

'Good morning,' a cool voice said directly behind them, and Jessica turned stiffly to find herself staring a long way up into Dane's expressionless face.

'Good morning,' she returned tritely, and if she had not known that it was medically impossible, she could have sworn that her heart did a quick somersault in her breast at the sight of him.

'I'm Dane Trafford,' he introduced himself with a faint smile in Megan's direction. 'What's your name?'

'Megan Leigh.' Blue eyes surveyed him a little shyly. 'Are you a doctor too?'

'I'm afraid so, yes.' His dark brows rose a fraction. 'Do you mind?'

'No,' Megan shook her head, taking in Jessica's taut features before she glanced up at Dane once more. 'Are you a friend of Dr Jessica's?'

Dane glanced briefly at Jessica, and those clever eyes did not miss that look of annoyance in her eyes, nor the embarrassed flush staining her cheeks.

'Don't pay any attention to the disapproving look on Jessica's face. She likes me, but she doesn't want anyone to know it,' he told Megan with a conspiratorial wink that made Jessica feel like kicking his shins. 'Would you like an ice-cream?' he changed the subject, surprising

Jessica with his offer.

'Oh, yes, please,' Megan accepted delightedly.

'Here, let me help you with some of those parcels,' Dane said at once, relieving Megan as well as Jessica of some of the excess weight they were carrying before they walked the short distance towards the tea room. 'My, but you have been doing a lot of shopping,' he observed dryly.

'Dr Jessica bought me a whole lot of new clothes to wear,' Megan told him proudly.

'Is that so?' he drawled, his mocking and faintly derisive glance meeting Jessica's as they entered the cool interior of the tea-room.

'There's an empty table over there,' Megan pointed excitedly.

'Then you lead the way, young Megan,' Dane replied and, with a mocking bow he added: 'After you, Dr Jessica.'

Jessica stepped past him in silence. Dane Trafford was really the most confusing and annoying man she had ever met, and she wondered what exactly he thought he was up to now.

'What will you have, Jessica?' he asked when they were seated, and that gleam of mockery was back in his eyes. 'An ice-cream?'

If he was trying to rattle her, then he was succeeding, she thought, but her voice was admirably calm when she said: 'I'll have tea, thank you.'

'Good,' he smiled faintly, and beckoning the waitress who stood hovering a little distance away, he placed their order. 'One large ice-cream for the little lady over there, and two teas, please,' he said, and when the waitress had departed he returned his attention to the child. 'Well, Megan, were you looking forward to your holiday here with Dr Jessica?'

'Oh, yes,' Megan smiled, and the smile lit up her eyes. 'Dr Jessica promised she would let me spend a holiday here with her, and she always keeps her promises.'

'Does she now?' he drawled lazily, flicking a mocking glance in Jessica's direction. 'Well, that's something worth remembering.'

'Are you a good doctor like Dr Jessica?' Megan questioned him directly, and Jessica felt that uncomfortable warmth stealing into her cheeks for the second time that morning.

'I hope I am, Dane replied evenly, but the eyes that met Jessica's were openly mocking. 'Am I a good doctor, would you say, Jessica?'

Sarcasm curved Jessica's lips into a mirthless smile. 'Would one question the abilities of a good computer?'

Megan glanced curiously from one to the other, not quite understanding, but aware of a certain undercurrent of animosity between these two adults, and Dane seemed to catch that look.

'What Dr Jessica means,' he explained to Megan, 'is that I'm a very good doctor. Perhaps even better than herself.' His glance was challenging now. 'That is what you meant, isn't it, Jessica?'

She hesitated, but when she glimpsed Megan's intent, questioning stare, she sighed and forced a smile to her lips. 'Could I have meant anything else?'

That mocking smile was back on Dane's lips, and she supposed that she ought to be thankful for that, but before he could say anything further, their tea and Megan's ice-cream was served to them.

The atmosphere relaxed slightly, and if Megan had been at all shy in Dane's company initially, then it evaporated swiftly under the influence of his charming personality. He *could* be charming, Jessica could not deny that, but the brand of charm he directed at Megan was free of that usual undertone of sensuality which he had applied towards Jessica so frequently in the past. She noticed, too, that he was good with children, and for some reason this surprised her. She had never imagined that a man like

Dane would show the slightest interest in children, except professionally, but she had obviously been mistaken.

Megan had never lacked in manners, and she thanked Dane very nicely for buying her an ice-cream when he eventually walked with them to where Jessica had parked her car, and he responded with, 'It was nice meeting you, Megan.'

With their parcels and the child safely in the Alfa, Jessica drew Dane aside and said sincerely, 'Thank you for being nice to her.'

'I can be very nice if you would only take the trouble to find out.'

His voice was a sensual caress, and Jessica was not quite sure whether to be thrilled or dismayed by it as she stared up at him with dark, contemplative eyes.

'We won't take up more of your time,' she said at length in a brisk voice. 'Thanks for the treat.'

'It was my pleasure,' he bowed mockingly.

As Jessica drove away she glanced in the rear view mirror to find Dane standing where she had left him and, almost as if he sensed her observation, he raised his hand in a final salute. Her cheeks flamed, and her pulse quickened and, putting her foot down harder on the accelerator, she drove away as quickly as possible.

'Damn the man!' she cursed him silently, but a part of her was relieved at the knowledge that he had not slammed the metaphorical door completely in her face.

'I like Dr Trafford,' Megan announced when they arrived back at the cottage with their parcels and, eyeing Jessica seriously, she asked: 'Don't you?'

'I—I suppose I do, yes,' Jessica replied with extreme caution.

'If you like him, then why did you look so cross when he started talking to us?' Megan demanded curiously.

'I wasn't cross,' Jessica protested lightly. 'I was just a little surprised.'

'Oh?'

Jessica could see that Megan was not quite sure what to make of that, and, to prevent further questioning, she organised the child into putting her new clothes away in the built-in cupboard of the guest room.

Vivien arrived shortly after lunch to collect Megan, and Jessica crossed her fingers childishly behind her back as she watched them drive away.

Jessica was called out only once that afternoon, but the rest of the time passed slowly, and wondering what was happening out at Mountain View was rather wearing on the nerves. It was almost time for Vivien and Megan to return when Jessica's telephone rang shrilly.

'Jessica?' Olivia's voice came clearly over the line. 'They have just left, and I thought you would like to know that Vivien behaved like a broody mother hen with a new chick. Frances seems to like Megan too, and I'd be surprised if your plan doesn't work.'

'Well, I'm certainly crossing my fingers and hoping for the best,' Jessica sighed. 'Megan is a lovely child.'

'You can say that again,' Olivia agreed wholeheartedly. 'If Vivien doesn't do something about her, then I'm tempted to adopt her myself.'

Jessica smiled to herself. 'You're too soft-hearted, Olivia.'

'Listen who's talking!' Olivia laughed softly, and their conversation ended moments later.

With Jessica being kept busy most of the time, it was inevitable that Vivien and Megan would become almost inseparable during the days that followed, and Vivien was most insistent that Megan sleep with them on those nights when Jessica was on call. Jessica protested, naturally, but not too much, and Megan quite happily took her toothbrush and her pyjamas up to the O'Brien house on those evenings when there was a possibility that Jessica might be called out to a patient.

During Megan's second week at Louisville, Jessica drove out to the forestry department with Dane one morning. This was a monthly ritual for Dane, but it was Jessica's first, and she looked forward to it with a degree of anticipation.

'On the whole,' Dane explained to her as they drove away from Louisville, 'the lumbermen are a fairly healthy lot, and who wouldn't be with all that sunshine and fresh air they enjoy?'

The clinic, however, was packed with patients that morning, and Dane took care of the men, while Jessica saw to the women and children. It was well into the afternoon before they drove away from there along the dusty road curving through the tall pines and gum trees, and Jessica felt pleasantly tired as she leaned back in her seat.

The Mustang was a fast car, and they reached the main road within a few minutes. The mountain pass lay ahead of them; a steep, winding road which was the gateway into the heart of the bushveld, and it was on one of those sharp, clearly defined bends that they encountered an empty cattle truck that had crashed through the safety railing to balance precariously over the edge of the road, but they were not the first to arrive on the scene of the accident. There were several cars parked just off the road, and people were milling about aimlessly as if they were not quite sure what to do.

'Am I glad to see you, Dr Trafford!' one man shouted, disengaging himself from the crowd and approaching them quickly. 'We need help. This man,' he pointed to the black man who was seated on the side of the road with his head in his hands, 'managed to jump out before the truck hit the railing, but the driver is still there in the cab, and we don't know whether he's alive or dead.'

'Get in your car and drive out to the Forestry Department as quickly as you can,' Dane rapped out the command while Jessica took her bag and approached the injured man. 'Tell them what's happened, and ask them to bring along a crane, or something with which to pull the truck back on to the road,' Jessica heard Dane instruct the man. 'And while you're there, get them to telephone the hospital in Louisville. We need an ambulance urgently.'

'I'm as good as there already,' the man said, and Jessica straightened from her examination as his car roared back the way they had come moments before.

'This man has a few minor lacerations and bruises,' Jessica explained as Dane approached her, 'but what about the one trapped in the cab?'

'I wish to hell I knew, but he'll have to wait until we have this truck back on the road,' Dane replied tersely, summing up the situation.

'I don't think it can wait,' Jessica told him quietly, opening up her medical bag and taking out whatever she might require to place it in the scarf which she had removed from about her throat.

'What do you think you're doing?' Dane demanded sharply when she had tied the knots securely and had slipped the scarf, with its contents, down the front of her blouse.

'I'm going to climb on to the back of that truck, and I think I'll be able to reach the cab that way,' she said, secretly thankful that she had chosen to wear slacks that morning. 'I've got to get to that man.'

'Are you crazy?' Dane demanded with incredulous harshness. 'That truck could go over that edge at the slightest puff of wind!'

'You know as well as I do that one of us has got to reach him, Dane, and I'm the obvious choice.'

'I'm damned if I'll allow it!' Dane exploded with a savagery that made her flinch inwardly, but her determination remained unaltered.

'For God's sake, Dane!' she cried anxiously. 'If he's not

dead already, then he could be bleeding to death!'

'Jessica, you're not risking your life——'

'I'd rather risk my life trying to save someone else's than stand here waiting and doing nothing.'

'I have a rope in my car,' one of the men who had stood around aimlessly interrupted their argument. 'We could tie it to the back of the truck and secure it to that tree on the opposite side of the road, and if we could motivate some of these people into warning oncoming traffic, then the rest of them could pack a few rocks on to the back of the truck which might just balance it to accommodate the lady's weight.'

Dane swung round to glare at the man. 'Now look here, I——'

'I like your suggestion,' Jessica interrupted hastily, 'but be quick about it.'

'I'll be as quick as I can, lady,' the man assured her, and somehow his activity and his issued commands spurred everyone into action.

'Do you know what you're doing?' Dane demanded of Jessica when she was finally given the signal that she could climb on to the truck.

'Yes, I do,' she replied grimly, looking up into steel-grey eyes narrowed against the sun.

'You're risking your life for someone who might already be dead.'

'I know, but I have to make sure.' She glanced contemplatively at the truck, then back at Dane. 'That truck is balanced too dangerously, Dane, to take your weight, and one of us has to go up there, you know that, don't you?'

'I know that, damn you, but——'

'Give me a hand up, and let's say no more,' she interrupted him urgently, and he looked oddly white about the mouth when he stepped towards her.

'In the name of heaven, Jessica, be careful,' he warned

hoarsely, and she nodded.

'I'll be careful.'

He lifted her from behind, his fingers biting into her flesh, and when her hands gripped the steel rails of the roofless cage on the back of the truck the vehicle swayed and creaked protestingly beneath her while she found a foothold. Dane shouted an order, his voice harsh, almost unrecognisable, and several more rocks joined those at the extreme end of the truck beneath her feet as she climbed over carefully. She was perspiring freely on that hot September afternoon, and she was more than a little frightened, but she had to reach that injured man in the cab. Slowly and carefully she moved across the dirty floor of the truck while rocks were added and the rope was tightened systematically. The smell of cow dung cloyed the air, but she barely noticed this as the truck swayed again, sending loose stones and gravel scattering down the sheer precipice, and the worst part was still to come. She had to climb over the railings directly behind the cab, and when she did so she found herself staring down into the gaping chasm beneath the suspended wheels of the truck. Nausea pushed up into her throat. She had never been able to stand heights, but there was no turning back now, and she had to go on.

She could hear Dane's voice as he shouted out instructions, but nothing registered at that moment as she clutched at the railings and placed a wary foot on the step beside the cab door. 'Don't look down!' she warned herself, and her hair clung to her damp forehead when her hand touched the handle and pushed it down. The door opened on dry, squeaking hinges, but it was with a measure of relief that she eased herself into the cab and seated herself gingerly on the seat beside the black man who lay slumped unconsciously over the steering wheel.

She closed the door, feeling more secure that way, then she turned to examine the man beside her. Blood was oozing freely from a cut against his temple, and there was a suggestion of blood on his lips, she noticed as her hands roamed expertly over his inert body, seeking further injuries.

'Jessica?' she heard Dane shouting her name.

'It's all right!' she shouted back. 'He's still alive!'

'Only just,' she muttered anxiously to herself, her eyes on the snapped steering wheel while her fingers sought the weak, fluttering pulse.

Quickly she removed the scarf with its precious contents from the inside of her blouse, and set to work. The minutes eased by slowly, but Jessica had lost all conception of time, and she was blessedly no longer aware of the danger she was in. She was concerned only for the welfare of her patient at that moment, and she thanked God that he was unconscious and oblivious of the pain.

'Hang on, will you,' Dane's voice reached her ears after what seemed like an eternity had passed. 'I can see the Forestry Department's crane coming up the road.' A few seconds later Jessica herself heard the sound of that great, labouring machine approaching them, and she heard, too, Dane's impatient, 'Hurry up, blast you!'

Jessica worked on steadily amidst the sound of shouted commands and running feet, pausing only to wipe the perspiration from her eyes. Help had arrived, and she hoped it would not be too late.

'Sit tight, Jessica,' Dane shouted down to her at last. 'They're going to haul the truck back on to the road, and the going might be rough.'

'Go ahead, I'm ready,' she shouted back and, bracing herself with her feet against the dashboard, she tried to hold the man beside her as steady as possible to prevent further injury from any jarring movements.

The strong smell of petrol was in her nostrils, and, as the truck began to move backwards steadily on to the road, her fear returned, and she shut her eyes tightly, sending up a silent prayer for their safety. The slightest spark could blast them into oblivion, and then all her efforts would have been in vain.

The truck groaned and creaked, slithered and swayed beneath her, then suddenly and miraculously, it was all over. The ambulance arrived with its sirens wailing, and the door beside her was wrenched open.

'Jessica!'

Her name was a hoarse cry from a man who was hardly recognisable as the suave, immaculate Dane Trafford with whom she had arrived on the scene of the accident. His face was white and wet with perspiration, and his white shirt was no longer white as it clung damply to his wide, muscled chest. His grey pants were covered in dust, and his fingers were shaking as they combed their way through his untidy hair. She wanted to touch him, to reassure him, but there was no time for that.

'You'll have to help me, Dane,' she spoke as matter-of-factly as possible. 'I managed to stop the external haemorrhaging, but he's unconscious and only barely alive.'

He nodded, and lifted her down off the truck in silence, his hands lingering momentarily at her waist, but when the ambulance men arrived he set her aside, and assisted them in lifting the patient on to the stretcher.

'I'll travel with him in the ambulance,' said Jessica, picking up her bag and following in the wake of the ambulance men.

'I'll see you at the hospital,' Dane replied tersely, and when Jessica climbed into the back of the ambulance, she had a brief glimpse of Dane striding towards his Mustang before the doors of the ambulance were shut securely.

CHAPTER SEVEN

TIME was Jessica's enemy. The man on the operating table had suffered multiple internal injuries, and the anaesthetist had warned that his pulse and respiratory system was growing weaker by the second. Five more minutes, that was all that she needed. *Just five more minutes!*

Dane was there, and his assistance was invaluable. They did not look at each other, and neither did they speak as they fought to save a man's life. The perspiration ran freely down the hollow of Jessica's back, and rose in tiny beads on her forehead which the Sister had wiped only a few seconds ago. Her gloved hands were steady as they worked with swift accuracy, stemming the flow of blood into the internal cavity, and repairing the damage to vital organs which had been pierced by crushed ribs, but time was running out much too fast.

'He's gone, Dr Neal.'

The anaesthetist's words, softly and sympathetically spoken, sliced through the tense silence in the theatre, and Jessica's hands stilled in the act of clamping off an artery. Time had won and, defeated, she turned away.

'Take over, Sister,' she heard Dane issue an abrupt instruction as she left the theatre and headed towards the washroom reserved for the female theatre staff.

Dane was following her for some reason, but she did not want to speak to him, and she quickened her steps. She needed to be alone, if only for a few minutes, to come to terms with what had occurred, and she hurriedly slipped into the washroom, closing the door firmly behind her.

She disposed of her theatre garments, peeling them off

one by one, but she was hardly aware of what she was doing. Where did she go wrong? she wondered as she stepped into the shower and turned the tap to allow the cold jet of water to beat against her heated skin. She tried to go over the operation, step by step, but her numbed brain refused to co-operate, and it was only when she removed her clothes off the hook behind the door of the cubicle that the stark reality of what had happened shocked her back to normal. Congealed blood stained her slacks and blouse, and it acted as a mocking reminder of her futile efforts. If only she had had more time! *If only!*

Dane barred her way when she finally emerged from the washroom. He was still dressed in his theatre garb, and his expression was inscrutable as he asked, 'Are you all right?'

'I'm fine,' she managed through stiff lips, lowering her gaze to the mask which he had pulled down to beneath his square jaw.

'These things happen, Jessica.'

'I know,' she smiled wanly.

'You did everything humanly possible.'

'Yes.' Tears welled up in her throat, but she swallowed them down convulsively and looked away. 'Well, I'd better fill in the necessary documents and see it that the next of kin are informed.'

'Jessica . . .' His hand gripped her shoulder, preventing her from leaving. 'Don't ever risk your life like that again.'

Their eyes met, and for a brief instant they were both reliving those frightening minutes she had spent in the truck with its front wheels suspended over the edge of the mountain road. It was something shared which made her feel oddly close to him at that moment, but his eyes became shuttered before her glance could define the unfathomable expression in them and, sighing, she shrugged off his hand.

'Goodnight, Dane.'

She felt his eyes following her down the passage until she turned the corner, but she dared not look back. Tears stung her eyes and hovered on her lashes, and she did not want him to see her disposing of them.

When the local newspaper emerged hot from the press the following morning, there was a long article on what they termed Jessica's 'Heroic deed', but Jessica herself barely glanced at it. There had been nothing heroic in what she had done. She had gone to the aid of a man in need, and he had died beneath her scalpel. She had failed in her attempts to save a life, and there was nothing heroic about that, she thought bitterly. Wherever she went that day people seemed to want to discuss the incident until she felt very much like screaming at them to 'Shut up!'

Two evenings later Jessica answered a knock on her front door to find Dane standing on her doorstep with that familiar mocking smile curving his mouth.

'Don't tell me,' she said with a hint of mockery to match his. 'You were passing, and when you saw my light was still on you thought you'd drop in for a cup of coffee.'

His expression remained unaltered as he stepped inside, but there was a suspicion of sardonic amusement in his voice when he asked: 'Have you taken to reading my mind, Jessica?'

'Heaven forbid that I should ever do that,' she exclaimed, closing the door and leading the way into the kitchen. 'I'll put the kettle on.'

'Is Megan asleep?' he asked, watching her spoon coffee into the cups.

'Yes, but not here,' Jessica replied without turning. 'When I'm on call she spends the night with Vivien and Peter.'

'I see.' He pulled out a chair from beneath the table and sat down, and it was not until she placed his coffee in front of him that he spoke again. 'It seems to me that

Megan has spent more time with Vivien than with you during her two week holiday.'

'Well, I'm not always around, and Vivien is fond of children, so it's sort of solved the problem of what to do with Megan while I'm out during the day, and often the night.'

'How very convenient!'

His expression was cynical, and she frowned as she seated herself opposite him. 'What are you getting at, Dane?'

'I think Megan was brought here with a purpose in mind.'

'Do you?' she asked cautiously.

'I do, yes,' he smiled faintly. 'Vivien and Peter haven't any children of their own, and Megan hasn't any parents. Put them together, and you could have quite a nice ready-made family.'

'Dane . . .'

'It's typical of a woman in the medical profession to allow her emotions to rule instead of her head,' he accused, but on this occasion she did not pay heed to the jibe, only the fear of what he might do.

'Dane, I——'

'I shan't say a word, if that's what you're afraid of,' he interrupted with that uncanny knack of reading her mind at times. 'I needed to have my suspicions confirmed, though.'

Jessica shifted a little uneasily in her chair. 'How did you guess?'

'It was simple,' he smiled mockingly. 'When Peter wasn't discussing some or other case, he was discussing Megan and the times they had spent together, and it made me wonder just how much time Megan has actually spent with you. One thing led to another, and there you have it.'

'It would be a marvellous solution, and you must admit it,' she argued.

'Sure, I admit it, but you must remember that you

can't always manipulate people in the direction your emotional heart dictates.'

He was right, of course, but at that precise moment she hated him for it, and she said stubbornly, 'I'm still hoping for the best.'

'How like a woman,' he mocked her, draining his cup and pushing it a little away from him to make room for his elbows on the table. 'What happens if your clever little plan fails?'

'I shall be disappointed, naturally.'

'And poor little Megan will be packed on to the train and sent back to her orphanage like an unwanted parcel.'

'Don't say it like that!' she protested, wincing inwardly as he placed a brutal finger on a sensitive spot.

'Face facts, Jessica,' he said harshly. 'You've given her a taste of freedom; of home life as she had known it once before, and it's going to be a damnable adjustment for her to have to return to that orphanage with its impersonal atmosphere.'

'For God's sake, stop it!' she cried huskily, jumping to her feet and turning her back on him to stare out of the window into the darkened garden beyond with unseeing eyes.

'You didn't think of that, did you?' he persisted cynically.

'I've thought of that, and much, *much* more!' she retorted hotly, swinging round to face him, but clutching at the cupboard behind her for support when she found him standing directly in front of her. 'If this fails, then I'm the one who'll bear the burden of guilt, and no one else.'

His mouth twisted cynically. 'I'm glad you said that, because I for one won't be sharing it with you.'

'I never expected anyone to share my burden, and I certainly wouldn't expect it of you,' she announced sharply, her heart beating so hard and fast that it was becoming difficult to speak.

'You're beautiful when you're angry.'

'Oh, shut up!' she exclaimed, the husky note in her voice becoming more pronounced. 'Go away, and leave me in peace.'

'Can I help it if your conscience is worrying you?'

She raised her chin defiantly. 'My conscience is quite clear.'

'Is it?'

There was a look in his eyes that filled her with uneasiness, and she said quickly, 'If you don't go now, I'll——'

His mouth came down to silence hers, parting her lips in a sensually arousing kiss, and his hand was curved about the nape of her neck when she would have drawn back. She tried not to respond, but an aching need rose within her when his free hand moved across her back to mould her to his lean, muscled body, and her own hands rose to explore the hair-roughened warmth of his chest where his shirt buttons had come undone. She felt the hard, steady beat of his heart quicken beneath her palm, then she was crushed against him, and her body was being explored with a freedom she had neither the strength, nor the will to deny him. His clever, supple hands did not lack experience, and her breasts grew taut with desire beneath those probing, caressing fingers. Her mind told her that she was playing with fire when she pressed closer to him still and slipped her arms about his strong neck, but her body seemed to have a will of its own. It was only when he raised his lips from hers that sanity returned with painful swiftness.

'You were saying?' he questioned mockingly, and a hot wave of shame and humiliation swept through her, making her struggle free of his arms to put some distance between them.

'I—I think you'd better go,' she managed thickly, trying desperately to control the trembling of her body, and it did not help when he came up behind her to grip her shoulders and draw her back against his hard chest.

'Must I go?' he demanded in a vibrantly sensual voice as he nibbled at the sensitive areas around her ear.

Tremors of unheard-of delight rippled through her, and her limbs weakened with an aching desire that made her lean back against him limply. Dane's soft, throaty laughter made her realise how totally he was in command of the situation. He knew exactly what he was doing to her, and for this reason alone she dared not give in.

'Please, Dane,' she begged, emotion deepening the huskiness in her voice. 'Please . . . don't do this to me.'

'Ah, well,' he sighed with that hateful hint of mockery in his voice and it was there in his eyes too when he swung her round and kissed her briefly on her soft, trembling mouth. 'It was worth a try.'

When the front door closed behind him moments later, Jessica was still standing where he had left her. She was shaking to such an extent that she had to grip the back of the upright, wooden chair for support, and in her heart she despised herself for being so weak. She loved him, yes, but that was no excuse, and she shrank inwardly when she tried to imagine what he must be thinking of her. She had no intention of stepping into the shoes of someone like Sylvia Summers, and unless she practised more control over her emotions in future, Dane might begin to imagine the opposite.

Jessica was kept too busy during the next few days to think much about her emotional problems, but she could not forget their conversation concerning Megan, and her uneasiness increased every time she thought of it. What if her plans failed, as Dane had suggested? What then?

She shook herself free of these thoughts, but they returned with a vengeance on Megan's last evening before she had to return to Johannesburg. They had shared a silent meal in the kitchen of her cottage, and afterwards, when they had washed the dishes and tidied the kitchen, Jessica sat down on a chair beside the table, and drew Megan to her side.

'You've been rather glum all evening,' she began tenderly, forcing a smile to her lips as she slipped an arm about the child. 'What's wrong?'

'I'm leaving tomorrow,' Megan said simply, and without hesitation, her blue eyes shadowed and her small mouth quivering in a way that made Jessica's heart ache for her.

'Did you enjoy your holiday?'

'Oh, yes, but . . .' Megan's eyes filled with tears, 'I wish I could stay here always.'

That knife turned in Jessica's heart, and she lifted Megan on to her lap to hug her close and comfort her.

'What did you like most about your holiday?' she asked when Megan's tears began to subside.

'Oh, everything,' Megan replied with a quivering sigh. 'I like Frances. She's a really super friend, and we're going to write to each other, and . . .' There was a contemplative pause before Megan continued. 'I like Aunty Vivien and Uncle Peter very much, and, next to my own mummy and daddy, they're just the best.'

'Do you really think so?'

Megan nodded her fair head against Jessica's shoulder and tightened her arms about Jessica's neck. 'I wish I didn't have to go back to that orphanage. I'm going to miss them, and I'm going to miss you too.'

'You're a darling, Megan,' Jessica whispered, hugging the child close to her, and hoping that the tears in her own eyes would go unnoticed.

A half hour later, with Megan safely tucked up in bed, Jessica slipped out the kitchen door and made her way through the moonlit garden towards Peter O'Brien's house. She had not formulated anything in her mind, and she had, as yet, no idea what she was going to say to him, but she knew that she could not leave things as they were.

There was a light on in Peter's study, and the sliding glass doors which led out on to the terrace stood open. Jessica hurried up the steps, her soft-soled shoes making no noise, but, at the sound of voices coming from the study, she paused and moved quickly into the shadows.

From her position out on the terrace she had a clear view into the study, and what she saw there held her motionless. Vivien was in Peter's arms, and it looked as if she was weeping uncontrollably.

Vivien in tears was such an unfamiliar sight that it was damn near unthinkable, and Jessica shrank farther into the shadows when she saw Peter lower his head towards Vivien's and murmur something to her.

'I can't let her go back, Peter,' Vivien's sobbing reply reached Jessica's ears. 'I just can't!'

Jessica turned away silently, but hope flared in her heart as she quickly made her way back to the cottage. Vivien could only have been referring to Megan, and, if Jessica was correct, then she would not be at all surprised if she found herself entertaining visitors that evening.

Less than a half hour later there was a knock on the kitchen door, and Jessica felt excitement churn through her as she put the lid on the teapot before opening the door.

'Come in,' she smiled at the two people standing on the doorstep. 'I've just made a pot of tea, and I could do with some company.'

'We'll have it here in the kitchen with you,' said Peter, making it clear that there was no ceremony involved in their visit.

'If you'd like,' Jessica nodded, setting out the cups and pouring out the tea while her guests seated themselves at the kitchen table.

Vivien had obviously repaired the damage caused by her recent tears, but she could not quite conceal the tremor in her hands when Jessica handed her her tea, and there was an awkward little silence before Vivien spoke.

'Jessica . . .' she began in a halting voice which was quite unlike her. 'About Megan.'

'What about Megan?' Jessica prompted in a controlled, casual voice which belied the excitement quivering within her.

'We'd like to adopt her,' Peter announced before Vivien could reply.

'Oh!' the sound came out almost like a sigh of relief, but Peter and Vivien were totally unaware of this.

'There's no one who could lay claim to her, is there?' Vivien asked anxiously. 'I mean . . . a distant relative, or something like that?'

Jessica shook her head. 'There's no one, Vivien.'

'In that case I don't foresee any problems,' Peter smiled broadly at his wife.

'We shall have to talk to Megan first, though,' Vivien suggested sensibly. 'She might not like the idea of being adopted by us.'

'I'll call her,' Jessica smiled at them, 'and if I know Megan then she should still be awake.'

'Before you do that, Jessica, I think we'd better tell you exactly what we have in mind,' Peter stopped her before she could reach the door. 'We don't want her to return to Johannesburg tomorrow. She could do her final term at the school here in Louisville.'

'I'm certain that it could be arranged,' said Jessica, and a smile once again lifted the corners of her mouth. 'My father knows all the right people, and he can be very persuasive when he puts his mind to it.'

Vivien and Peter glanced at each other with a new eagerness in their eyes, then Vivien looked up at Jessica and said: 'Could we talk to Megan now?'

'I'll bring her here to you,' Jessica replied, and moments later she was bending low over the child. 'Megan darling,

I'm glad you're still awake. Uncle Peter and Aunty Vivien are here, and they would like to talk to you.'

Megan fired questions at Jessica while being helped into her dressing gown and slippers, but Jessica told her calmly that she would soon know what it was all about, and taking her by the hand she led her into the kitchen where Peter and Vivien were waiting anxiously.

They stared at Megan in silence for a moment, and Megan stared back solemnly, then Vivien glanced enquiringly at her husband. 'Peter?'

'I'll leave it to you, darling,' he smiled amiably.

'Come here, Megan,' Vivien said quietly, holding out her hands, and Megan went to her at once, placing her small hands in Vivien's. 'How would you like to stay here with us?' Vivien asked, barely able to conceal her excitement.

'With—with you and Uncle Peter, you mean?' Megan questioned hesitantly.

'Yes, Vivien nodded.

'For good?' Megan asked, her blue eyes widening.

'Yes,' Vivien nodded again. 'We would very much like you to be our own little girl.'

Jessica could see that Megan was finding it difficult to believe her ears, and her heart ached for the child as Megan asked, 'You want to adopt me?'

'Yes, but——' Vivien halted with a measure of uncertainty in her dark glance, 'only if you would want that too.'

Tears sprang into Megan's eyes and, flinging herself into Vivien's arms, she cried, 'Oh, yes, yes, please!'

'Megan! Oh, Megan!' There were tears in Vivien's eyes now as she held the child close, and laid her cheek against those fair curls, but this time they were tears of happiness. 'It's going to make such a wonderful difference to our lives having you with us.'

Tears rose in Jessica's throat and stung her eyelids as

she took in the happy picture before her, but she hastily blinked her tears away when she caught Peter's blue gaze resting on her speculatively.

'Does this mean that I don't have to go back to Johannesburg tomorrow?' Megan was asking.

'You're going to stay right here with us from now on,' Peter replied firmly.

'Yippee!' Megan exclaimed excitedly through her tears. 'Oh, I love you Aunty Vivien, and you too, Uncle Peter!'

She hugged them both in turn, and everyone seemed to be talking at the same time until Vivien said firmly, 'You'd better get back to bed now, Megan, but I'll be here in the morning to take all your things up to our house.'

'All right,' Megan nodded obediently, her eyes shining stars of happiness. 'Goodnight, and ... thank you for wanting me.'

That was almost too much for Jessica and, turning away, she swallowed convulsively at the lump in her throat.

'I'm so happy I could cry,' Vivien announced after Megan had gone back to bed.

'Oh, no, you don't,' Peter warned laughingly. 'You've done enough of that for one night.'

'Yes, I suppose I have,' Vivien admitted, wiping the telltale moisture from her eyes with the tips of her fingers. 'Sorry, darling.'

Peter O'Brien eased his lean body out of the chair to draw his wife to her feet and into his arms, and Jessica turned away once again from the intimate scene before her to give them a moment's privacy.

'I'll telephone my father this evening,' she said eventually, 'and he should have an affirmative answer for us first thing in the morning.'

'You're very sure of his powers of persuasion, then?' Peter questioned her with a quizzical smile.

'Very sure,' Jessica smiled back at him.

'Then we'll leave it all in your hands, Jessica,' he said and, taking Vivien by the arm, he ushered her towards the door.

They said goodnight and when the door closed behind them Jessica could almost have leapt for joy, but she restrained herself and hurried into the lounge instead to telephone her father.

If Jonathan Neal was surprised at his daughter's request, then he gave no indication of it over the telephone, and merely promised to let her know as soon as he had spoken to the authorities concerned.

Jessica was almost too relieved and excited to sleep that night, but she somehow managed to fall asleep towards midnight. Vivien, true to her word, arrived very early the following morning to collect Megan, and Jessica had barely walked into her consulting-room when her father's call came through.

'It's all in order, Jessica,' he said. 'The adoption papers will be drawn up, and posted as soon as possible to your local magistrate.'

Jessica confronted Peter with this news a few minutes later, and a look of intense relief flashed across his lean face.

'Thank you, Jessica,' he smiled, leaning back into his chair, and then that speculative look entered his eyes once more. 'You didn't seem at all surprised last night when we confronted you with the news that we wanted to adopt Megan.'

It was not a question but a statement, and Jessica replied to it truthfully. 'In an unguarded moment, after the birth of Olivia's baby, Vivien made me aware of her need for a child of her own, so . . .'

'So you brought Megan into our lives with a purpose,' he finished for her when she paused, and she saw a look of understanding enter his eyes.

'I took a desperate gamble, and I knew that if it paid off it would make three people very happy.'

'You're a remarkable young woman, Dr Jessica Neal,' Peter announced, then he rose from behind his desk and turned to face the window, but not before she had glimpsed something almost like tears in his eyes. He was silent for so long that Jessica did not know whether to stay or go, then he started speaking once again, and his voice was thick with emotion. 'For years now Vivien and I have pretended to each other, *and* to others, that it made no difference to us whether we had children, or not, and we succeeded admirably, I think, until Megan Leigh walked into our lives with her beguiling blue eyes and curly fair hair. It took one smile, directed like a well-aimed arrow at our most vulnerable spot, to make us aware once again of the emptiness in our otherwise full lives.' Peter turned and smiled crookedly at Jessica. 'Everyone loved Megan from the moment they set eyes on her, and she blended into our family as if she had been there all her life.' He looked away a little selfconsciously. 'I don't quite know how to thank you, Jessica.'

'Don't thank me,' she said quickly, placing a light hand on his arm. 'I would be most embarrassed if you did.'

Before he could say anything further, she left his consulting-room and returned to her own. She had not felt so happy in a long time, nor so relieved, and not even Dane's snide remarks later that day could banish entirely that contented feeling brought on by the success of her venture.

'Dr Jessica Neal, the worker of miracles,' he said. 'You waved your magic wand, and everything worked out well towards the climax where they all lived happily ever after.'

'You share in their happiness, don't you, Dane?'

'Oh, sure I do,' he smiled cynically, 'but thank your lucky stars that it worked out this way, or one very unhappy child would have been on her way back to a life she hated.'

'I do thank my lucky stars,' Jessica said quietly, her dark gaze unfaltering as it met his. 'I'm grateful, too, that you won't have the opportunity of saying "I told you so".'

His mouth tightened, 'You misunderstand me, Jessica. I don't belittle what you've accomplished, but there was a risk involved which could have led to a great deal of unhappiness.'

'I realise that, and don't think I haven't spent sleepless nights wondering whether I'd done the right thing,' she replied angrily. 'I've tormented myself with the possibility that this venture might fail, but it hasn't, and I'm grateful for it, so I'd thank you to keep your cynical remarks to yourself.'

'It's your job as a physician to look after the *physical* wellbeing of your patients, and not their *personal* wellbeing,' he told her with a distinct sneer on his lips. 'If you're going to become emotionally involved with your patients in future, then I suggest you give up practising medicine and sit yourself down behind a desk as a psychologist and guidance counsellor.'

'You know something?' she snapped back furiously. 'I might just do that!'

They glared at each other in silence, then his hands gripped her wrists and she was jerked up against him with a force which nearly succeeded in robbing her of breath.

'Do you know something, Jessica?' he smiled down at her with that gleam of mockery in his eyes. 'You're really most desirable when you're angry.'

Her lips parted to berate him, but he lowered his head swiftly to cover her mouth with his, and she was momentarily lost in the sensual expertise of his lingering kiss. When she tried to escape him, his hands merely tightened on her wrists, and her arms were twisted behind her back to render her helpless. 'Don't respond!' her mind warned, but her treacherous body was already melting against his.

His lips travelled down the column of her throat to where her pulse was beating erratically, then they moved upwards once again to tease and tantalise the corners of her quivering, responsive mouth until she ached with the need to feel his lips against her own.

Dane released her abruptly when there was a knock on the door, and Jessica turned away to hide her flushed cheeks when Sister Hansen entered the room.

'Aren't the two of you going home tonight?' she demanded as she marched across the room to collect the files on Jessica's desk.

'We were just leaving,' Dane announced with a calmness Jessica envied at that moment while she struggled to control the wild beat of her heart.

'It's just as well you're still here, though,' Sister Hansen remarked in her brisk voice. 'The hospital telephoned, Dr Trafford. They'd like you to call on Mrs le Roux. She's complaining of chest pains and difficulty in breathing.'

'I'm on my way,' Dane replied, striding towards the door where he paused briefly to cast a glance in Jessica's direction. 'See you later.'

'Not if I can help it,' Jessica told herself silently as the door closed behind him and, turning, her glance met Sister Hansen's speculative stare.

'You're just a little thing,' the older woman said, 'but in the three months you have been here, you have made your mark. You have won everyone's admiration and respect, and there are going to be plenty of unhappy faces around when your year is up here in this bushveld town.'

'I've only done my job to the best of my ability,' Jessica muttered selfconsciously, checking the contents of her medical bag and snapping it shut.

'You do more than most doctors,' Emily Hansen

argued. 'You care about your patients not only as patients, but as people, and that's where the difference comes in. Take Dr O'Brien for instance———'

'Dr O'Brien is a marvellous doctor,' Jessica interrupted in defence of a man she had come to admire.

'I don't argue that point,' Sister Hansen smiled, 'but look what you've done for him. I've never seen him look as happy and contented as he did today. Oh, we all knew about his wife not being able to have children, but no one ever mentioned it, and while it didn't seem to matter to them, no one bothered. You came, however, and saw their need, but most important of all, you did something about it instead of letting it pass you by.'

'Sister Hansen, you flatter me unnecessarily,' Jessica told her seriously. 'Circumstances were in my favour, or I might not have done anything about it either. One can't just walk up to people and say, "Would you like to adopt a child?". They would most probably tell you to mind your own business, and rightly so, but I happened to have a little friend like Megan Leigh whose need matched theirs, and the rest came about naturally.'

'I still think that what you did was wonderful,' Sister Hansen stated firmly, 'and I shan't change my mind about that.'

Having said her piece, the older woman marched out of the room, but Jessica remained a few minutes longer to tidy her desk before going home. She felt a little embarrassed by Sister Hansen's praise, but she could not help wishing that Dane had been a little less critical of her actions.

CHAPTER EIGHT

JESSICA was called away from her hospital rounds one morning a week later, and the message she received was that she should return to the consulting-rooms at once. Realising that Peter would not have interrupted her rounds unless it was something urgent, she drove away from the hospital at a speed which she hoped would go unnoticed by the traffic department. Ten minutes later she was joining an equally puzzled Dane in Peter's consulting-room.

'I've had a call from the district nurse at a small settlement in northern Venda,' Peter explained without further delay. 'Chief Cedric Kapufu needs immediate medical attention, and because of his age the district nurse considered it unwise to move him to the clinic ten kilometres from his home.'

'Any idea what's wrong?' Dane questioned abruptly.

'The district nurse suspects appendicitis, but she can't say for sure,' Peter replied, a frown drawing his brows together. 'It sounds rough, so I suggest you take Jessica along with you.'

'It will take us two, maybe three hours by car,' Dane remarked thoughtfully. 'You know what those roads are like.'

'I'd ask Bernard to fly you there, but his plane is a two-seater.'

'I could fly us there, if Bernard will entrust his aircraft to me,' Jessica spoke for the first time, and the two men glanced at her with a mixture of astonishment and surprise.

'You can fly an aeroplane?' Dane demanded with typical cynicism.

'I have a pilot's licence, if you'd like to see it,' Jessica hit back sarcastically.

'I'll ring through to Mountain View,' Peter intervened. 'If Bernard isn't there then Olivia will get a message through to him.'

Peter did not waste any time getting through to the farm, and a few minutes later he was replacing the receiver and turning to face them with a satisfied smile on his lean face.

'Bernard will have the plane ready and waiting for you when you arrive at Mountain View, and while you're on your way there I'll telephone the district nurse to let her know you're coming so that she can make the necessary arrangements.'

'Then let's waste no more time standing around here,' Dane said briskly, and he strode towards the door with Jessica following close behind him.

Dane's Mustang and Jessica's Alfa arrived almost simultaneously at Mountain View's airstrip where Bernard awaited them. The red and white Cessna stood out on the runway and, realising the urgency of their mission, Bernard wasted no time in discussing the details of their flight with Jessica, advising her on the best air route to take while Dane looked on with cynical uncertainty.

'Cheer up, Dane,' Bernard laughed at length, slapping Dane on the back in a friendly, amused manner. 'If Jessica can fly as knowledgeably as she talks, then you're in safe hands.'

Dane grimaced. 'I can think of safer places to be at this moment.'

'Coward!' Jessica mocked him.

'I admit it,' Dane smiled wryly. 'With a woman manning the controls one can expect anything.'

Jessica chose to ignore this and, turning towards Bernard, she held out her hand. 'Thanks very much. We appreciate your help.'

'My pleasure,' he smiled, clasping her hand briefly but firmly.

Jessica walked purposefully towards the Cessna, and Dane followed with an audible sigh. She climbed into the seat behind the controls, blessing the fact that she wore sensible shoes and a wide, accommodating skirt, and Dane climbed up after her into the passenger seat. He closed the door for her, and they belted themselves in before she put on the earphones and passed the spare set to Dane.

'I hope you know what you're doing,' Dane remarked cynically as he watched her flick switches and turn the appropriate dials.

'Relax, Dane,' she laughed. 'I'll get you there in one piece.'

'Dead or alive?' he queried caustically.

'Alive, I hope,' she told him. 'Now, shut up, will you?'

The engine sprang to life, and the Cessna vibrated beneath them while Jessica made radio contact with the nearest air base. Moments later they were taxiing along the runway, and a thrill of excitement churned through Jessica as she increased engine power. She had opened up the throttle, and the Cessna leapt forward with increasing speed, then she pulled back the stick, and the ground seemed to fall away beneath them as they climbed smoothly into the blue, cloudless sky.

'Hm . . .' Dane grunted. 'Not bad.'

Jessica was too exhilarated at being able to fly again to care what Dane thought at that moment. For one who did not care much for heights, she had taken to piloting an aircraft like a duck to water and, to date, she had logged up several hundred flying hours.

It was a perfect day for flying, she decided, swinging the plane in a north-easterly direction, and if all went well they should reach their destination within a half hour.

'Do they have an operating theatre at the clinic?' she broke the silence between Dane and herself.

'Not that I know of, but I guess they have certain facilities for emergencies.'

'What if the patient can't be moved?'

'Then we'll operate on the spot.'

A mocking smile curved her mouth. 'You've brought your emergency theatre along with you, then?'

'What's that supposed to mean?' he demanded, his voice sounding unexpectedly harsh in her ears. 'You know damn well we might have no choice but to operate, regardless of the primitive conditions.'

'Yes, I know.' She removed her eyes from the controls and met his angry glance. 'I was merely throwing your own words back at you, but without much success.'

'I get it.' His mouth tightened. 'You're referring to the time I berated you for not taking Olivia through to the hospital, is that it?'

She averted her glance. 'That's correct.'

'The circumstances are different in this instance.'

'There's no difference in what you might have to do, and in what I had to do for Olivia,' she argued. 'In fact, the risks are even greater in this case.'

'We won't argue about that,' he said abruptly, and annoyingly.

'No, of course not.'

'Now you're sulking,' Dane eventually broke the uncomfortable silence between them which had been filled only with the steady drone of the Cessna's engine.

'I'm not sulking, Dane,' she sighed. 'I was merely trying to fathom your reasoning.'

'It's really quite simple,' he explained with a tolerance which merely increased her annoyance. 'When there's an emergency such as this, then you make do with what you have.'

'Exactly,' she snapped.

'Well then, what's the problem?'

'The birth of Olivia's baby was an emergency of its

own kind, and I made do with what I had, so I fail to see why you were so angry about it at the time.'

'A man can keep a clear head at a time like that, but a woman . . .'

'Oh, not that again!' Jessica laughed despite her anger. 'You disappoint me, Dane. I never would have taken you for someone with chauvinistic tendencies.'

'I guess every man has a bit of chauvinism tucked away somewhere in his make-up, but that's not what I'm getting at.' He gestured disparagingly with his hands. 'Women tend to approach things from an emotional angle, and you're a fine example of that.'

Jessica was silent for a moment, staring resolutely ahead of her, then she said coldly, 'If my hands weren't occupied at this moment, Dane, I'd strike you.'

Dane laughed softly. 'You have such lovely hands, Jessica, and I shall enjoy their touch whether it be in anger, or passion.'

'I suggest you help me look for the landing strip near the clinic,' she changed the subject, flashing him an angry glance when she suspected that he had baited her deliberately. 'We should be able to see it any minute now.'

Ten minutes later Jessica executed a perfect landing on the airstrip in Venda, and when they climbed out of the Cessna, carrying their medical bags, a black man of obvious importance came towards them. He introduced himself as Patrick Kapufu, the brother of their patient, and without further delay they were driven to the Chief's home in a long black limousine which smacked of wealth.

Jessica was not quite sure what she had envisaged, but she certainly had not expected someone as important as Chief Cedric to be lying on a grass mat spread out on the floor of a square mud hut which had been partitioned off into four sections; the living quarters, kitchen, and presumably two bedrooms. It was primitive but clean, and the thatched roof kept the interior cool despite the heat outside.

Chief Cedric had the appearance of a man who ate hearty meals and suffered the consequences gladly. He was totally overweight, and at that moment he was writhing on the floor in obvious agony. A black woman in a blue uniform stepped forward to introduce herself as Sister Ravele, the district nurse for that area, and together they approached the patient.

'The pain, Doctor!' the Chief groaned, recognising Dane at once when he and Jessica kneeled down beside him. 'It is terrible, this pain.'

'I can well imagine it is, Chief,' Dane announced bluntly, making a swift but thorough examination, and confirming the district nurse's diagnosis.

'Who is this woman?' Chief Cedric asked Dane, his hand gesturing wearily towards Jessica. 'She is your wife?'

'No, Chief,' Dane grinned, his mocking glance resting on Jessica. 'I'm not married, and this is Dr Neal who has come to assist me.'

'A man must have a wife,' Chief Cedric grunted feverishly, clutching his stomach, but Dane and Jessica were already moving away from his side and gesturing the district nurse to follow them.

'What are you going to do, Dane?' Jessica asked unnecessarily as she glanced up into his grim face.

'We can't move him. There isn't time, and it would be a hellish journey for someone in his condition.'

Jessica cast her glance into the room they had just left, but when she turned back to Dane there was something close to horror in her dark eyes. 'You're going to operate right here?'

'I have no choice,' he said abruptly, then he turned towards Sister Ravele to issue brisk instructions. 'Get someone to help you. We need a table to accomodate the

Chief, a lead-light, water to scrub in, and plenty of disinfectant.'

Sister Ravele carried out Dane's instructions with surprising swiftness, while the Chief's brother provided the lead-light which he connected to the battery of his car. The Chief was a big man, and it took eight of them to blanket-lift him on to the long, narrow table. Jessica and Dane scrubbed and checked through the sterilised instruments they had brought with them while Sister Ravele prepared the patient for surgery.

The Chief's black, pain-filled eyes met Dane's when they finally stood around the improvised operating table. 'Make me well, Doctor, and I will give you ten cattle to pay for the woman you want.'

The Chief was nothing if not persistent, Jessica thought, suppressing a smile, but Dane's expression remained inscrutable.

'Our customs are different, Chief Cedric, you must know that,' Dane told him as he checked the light dangling from the rafters.

'No different,' the Chief muttered stubbornly. 'A man must have a wife . . .' he continued and, casting a glance in Jessica's direction, he added: 'And woman must have a man. It is written so.'

'No more talking, Chief,' Dane instructed, casting a brief, mocking glance in Jessica's direction. 'We're going to put you to sleep now, and when you wake up you're going to feel much better.'

The Chief muttered something in his own language which only Sister Ravele seemed to understand, for she grinned broadly and cast a speculative glance in Jessica and Dane's direction, but Dane was oblivious of this as he nodded briefly at Jessica, indicating that she could give the anaesthetic.

Jessica found the vein in the Chief's arm, and injected pentothal sodium directly into it. Moments later she raised her glance. 'You can go ahead, Dane.'

'Ready, Sister Ravele?' Dane queried, and when the district nurse nodded, he said grimly, 'Here we go, then.'

Jessica had never worked under such primitive conditions before, but Dane looked calm and confident, his hands steady as he made the first incision down to the muscle. When the caecum was finally exposed they found the ruptured appendix, and then Dane had to work fast. Infected matter had been discharged into the peritoneal cavity, and suddenly it was no longer a simple appendectomy.

A little more than an hour later they were blanket-lifting the Chief into the adjoining room where Sister Ravele had prepared a bed for the patient, and leaving the Sister in charge, Dane and Jessica packed their bags and stepped out into the blinding afternoon sun.

'Are you leaving at once, Doctor?' Patrick Kapufu wanted to know after they had informed him of his brother's condition.

'We can't leave until we're sure the infection has cleared up, and that might not be until tomorrow.' Dane's reply shocked Jessica into realising that neither of them had thought to bring along a change of clothing, but then neither of them had expected complications to set in.

'That is good,' Patrick Kapufu's voice sliced through her thoughts. 'We are having a very important ceremony this evening, and we would be honoured if you would both attend. It is the *domba* dance which is performed by the young women preparing for marriage, or as the White people call it, the snake dance.'

Dane's taut features relaxed into a semblance of a smile. 'We would be honoured to be your guests.'

'Come,' Patrick ordered, 'I will show you to your huts.'

Jessica had no idea what Dane was thinking, but she viewed the night ahead in a mud hut with a great deal of trepidation. To her surprise the huts Patrick had mentioned were more like log cabins with a neatly thatched roof. Each was furnished with modern pine furniture, and added to this there was the luxury of a private bathroom.

Jessica's surprise must have been evident, for Patrick smiled at her obvious ignorance, and explained tolerantly, 'My brother, Chief Cedric, still prefers the old-fashioned and primitive way of life, but these huts were designed and furnished for the comfort of his guests.'

'I'm sure we shall be most comfortable,' Jessica assured him, a blush staining her cheeks. 'Thank you very much.'

'Shall I telephone Dr O'Brien and tell him that you're staying the night, Dr Trafford?' Patrick asked Dane.

Dane nodded curtly. 'I would be grateful if you would.'

'I have ordered one of my brother's wives to see to your needs, and I shall call for you personally as soon as the moon has risen,' Patrick told them. 'The festivities start only after dark.'

He bowed towards them, and then he was gone, leaving Jessica and Dane alone on the doorstep of her hut.

'It seems as though we have a few entertaining hours ahead of us,' Jessica remarked casually.

'Have you ever seen them do the snake dance before?' Dane asked, his eyes narrowed and faintly mocking.

'Briefly on film, yes,' she nodded. 'Have you?'

'I was privileged to watch it once soon after my arrival in Louisville, and it's something worth seeing twice.'

'I shall look forward to it, then,' she smiled up at him tentatively, but he was already turning from her and striding towards his own hut.

He looked as tired and hot as she felt and, sighing, she entered the hut and closed the door behind her.

Before she could do more than just take in her surroundings, there was a knock on the door, and she opened it to find herself presented with a plate of sandwiches and an iced lime drink on a small tray. Jessica thanked the woman, and white teeth flashed in the ebony-coloured face before she departed, leaving Jessica to enjoy her light meal. It did more than fill the hollow at the pit of her stomach, and afterwards she indulged in a cool, refreshing shower.

Leaving off her skirt and blouse, she decided to try out the bed. The mattress was soft, yielding beneath her tired body, and a few minutes later she was asleep.

Jessica had no idea how long she slept, but she awoke with a start to find Dane bending over her, and she was suddenly conscious of several things all at once. Her face was devoid of make-up, and her embarrassing state of undress was being observed by a pair of warm, sensually lazy eyes.

'Dinner is served,' he announced mockingly, taking in her flushed cheeks, and the thrust of her small breasts against the lacy top of her petticoat, and for one frightful moment she thought that he was referring to *her* as replenishment for *his* sexual appetite, but, almost as if he had read her thoughts, he added derisively, 'I told the Chief's wife not to disturb you, but to set a table for two in my hut.'

'Oh.' She breathed a little easier when he straightened and turned towards the door. 'I'll be with you in about ten minutes.'

'Make it five,' he said, opening the door and glancing back at her with eyes that took in every detail of her appearance once again. 'I don't enjoy cold steak.'

Jessica's heartbeats resumed their normal pace when the door closed behind him, and she dressed quickly. From the small purse which she always carried around with her she took out her comb, powder compact and lipstick, and two minutes later she grimaced at her reflection in the mirror. With no powder base or moisturiser handy, this would just have to do, she decided.

Dusk had settled over the heated, silent earth while they enjoyed the meal which had been prepared for them, but the silence around them seemed to be full of the promise of excitement.

When the rising moon shed its first silvery rays across the darkened, dense vegetation, Patrick arrived to escort them along the path leading towards the river where the fires had been lit in preparation for the ceremony.

Every year, from far and near, young maidens were sent to Chief Cedric's settlement to participate in this ritual, Patrick explained as he guided them towards a low bench a little distance from the fires. Tonight, he said, there would be approximately one hundred and fifty girls, the most there had ever been.

Jessica and Dane were not the only spectators. Almost the entire settlement was there, seating themselves in a large circle around the fires, and excitement shivered through Jessica when a sudden hush fell upon all the spectators. She glanced in the direction Patrick was pointing, and through an opening in the crowd stepped a tall man in a feathered headdress and splendid ceremonial robes.

'That's the Master of the *domba*,' Dane whispered to her, 'and *domba* means python, by the way.'

Jessica watched as he stepped into what would be termed the 'arena', and he was followed by the seemingly endless row of young girls, wearing beaded strips of cloth to cover their loins, and very little else. They filed into the arena, every last one of them, and then, at a given signal from the Master of the *domba*, they silently enacted something which Jessica found difficult to understand at first, but Patrick was quick to explain.

'When our young women are preparing for marriage, they attend lectures in the evenings, and they are taught many things about the morals and conventions of married life. They are also taught to mime the things they have been taught, and that is what they are doing now.'

'What makes the python so special; so significant?' Jessica asked in a curious whisper.

Patrick smiled with that tolerance she had noticed once

before. 'The python is a powerful snake, and among some of our more primitive people it is still considered a god.'

The miming continued for a considerable time before the drums started thudding, and this caused a stir of excitement to rise among the spectators as the Master of the *domba* cried out in a deep, melodious voice, '*Tharu ya mahbidighami!*'

'The python is uncoiling,' Patrick translated for them, and indeed it was.

The girls, all one hundred and fifty of them, joined up one behind the other until they formed what looked like a weaving, sinuous line to perform the dance of the python, and it was the most fascinating spectacle Jessica had ever witnessed. The girls, their dark, near-naked bodies gleaming in the light of the fires, performed the rhythmic, evocative motions of the python's lithe movement, while the baritone of the *mirumba* and the bass of the *ngoma* drums provided a primitive and intoxicating rhythm which seemed to stir the blood in Jessica's veins.

Caught up in the magic of this primitive ritual, she leaned back against Dane when she felt his arm slip about her waist, and the touch of his lips against her temple became a part of this unusual night.

Two hours later, when the fires had died down to glowing embers in the darkness, the exhausted dancers slipped away to rest, the drums ceased their rhythmic beat, and Patrick wished Dane and Jessica a peaceful night after escorting them part of the way back to their huts.

Under the spell of those primitive drums which seemed to continue beating within her, Jessica did not avoid Dane's descending lips in the shadows close to their huts. His hands caressed her, awakening new fires and wild emotions which made her cling to him in sheer rapture when he lifted her in his arms and carried her effortlessly into his hut. In the darkened intimacy of the room his lips and hands set her aflame with a desire which craved fulfilment, and there was no room for thought when he eventually peeled off her clothes, his hands brushing against her skin with a slow sensuality which sent exquisite sensations surging through her.

She had never dreamed that she could ever want a man as much as she wanted Dane at that moment, and her hands, eager to touch him as he was touching her, tugged at his shirt buttons. His breathing was as ragged as her own as he shrugged himself out of it hurriedly, his hand going to the buckle of his belt, and when at last he lowered her down on to the bed she surrendered herself willingly to the demands of those pursuasive hands on her responsive flesh. She was intoxicated by his kisses, her hand freely caressing his hair-roughened chest and muscled shoulders, and she gloried in the experience, but a little cry of intense pleasure escaped her when his mouth left hers to explore the most sensitive areas of her breast.

'Oh, Dane, Dane . . .' she moaned softly, her body aflame with the urgency of her desire as his hand slid down her abdomen to seek further intimacies, but at that moment there was an urgent knock on the door of the hut.

Shocked back to sanity, Jessica drew a sharp breath as if someone had struck her a vicious blow, but Dane's splayed fingers tightened on her hip as if in warning, and she knew why. Even in this day and age, with polygamy practised by the Venda chiefs, it was still unheard of that a man should lie down with a woman before going through the proper ritual of paying for her in the required manner with the accepted number of cattle, and if she and Dane should be found together it would be considered an insult to their imperious host.

'Yes? What is it?' Dane's abrupt voice scraped along her raw nerves.

'The Chief is running a fever,' Sister Ravele's voice reached them through the door. 'Will you come at once, Dr Trafford?'

'I'll be there as quick as I can,' Dane replied, and shame and humiliation washed over Jessica like a heated wave as they lay there in the darkness listening to her hurried footsteps disappearing in the direction of the Chief's hut. 'I'm sorry, Jessica,' Dane muttered thickly, and she was not quite sure whether he meant that he regretted the interruption, or the fact that he had tried to make love to her.

'You'd better go,' she told him in a shamed, stilted voice. 'I'll follow you after a few minutes.'

Jessica lay shivering in the blessed darkness despite the warmth of the night while Dane pulled on his clothes and left the hut. When the door closed behind him she slipped out of bed and dressed quickly, but her hands were shaking to such an extent that she could hardly fasten the buttons of her blouse. She went hot and cold alternatively at the thought of what might have happened had Sister Ravele not needed Dane at that precise moment, and she felt sick inside at the thought of her own senseless behaviour.

She slipped out of Dane's hut feeling very much like a criminal of sorts and, jumping at every moving shadow, she made her way towards the Chief's hut which was lit inside with a dim gas lamp.

She could not look at Dane, but neither did he look up when she entered the room, which reeked of disinfectant. She did not exist for him at that moment, except as someone to carry out his abrupt instructions, and she did so like an automaton, grateful for something to do which would prevent her from thinking about what had happened.

Jessica filled a syringe with an antibiotic and injected it into the patient's arm, then an awful waiting period followed while they watched over the Chief, observing his reaction to the drug with growing relief. It seemed like hours while they sat there beside his bed instead of forty-five minutes before Dane rose to his feet.

'I think we can all get some rest now,' he announced, his fingers on the Chief's pulse. 'The worst is over.'

'I'll stay with him a little longer, then I'll arrange for someone to take over from me,' Sister Ravele whispered, and Dane nodded his approval.

Jessica left the hut ahead of Dane, but his long, lithe strides brought him to her side before she had gone very far, then he matched his steps to her shorter ones, and they walked in silence through the shadows towards her hut. If only he would say something, *anything* to relieve the tension between them, but only the usual night sounds of the bush disturbed the silence, and the heavy, tormented beat of her own heart.

At the door of her hut she muttered a stilted 'goodnight', but his hands reached for her, and he would have drawn her against him had she not placed her hands against his hard chest to hold him off.

'No, Dane,' she said in a surprisingly cool voice as she strained back against the hands that held her. 'What happened earlier was a mistake I don't want to repeat.'

His hands tightened on her shoulders, his fingers biting into the soft flesh until she could have cried out with the agony of it. 'It was no mistake, Jessica. You wanted me as much as I wanted you.'

'I don't deny that,' she bit out the words, her body growing taut with resentment. 'But it was lust, nothing more, and I'm ashamed.'

He released her so unexpectedly that she staggered, and the height and breadth of him in the darkness was suddenly menacing as he demanded harshly, 'Do you mean that?'

There was something odd about Dane at that moment, a certain urgency which her tortured brain could not grasp, and she pushed trembling hands through her short, dark curls as she leaned back against the door frame for support.

'Yes,' she said at last in a tired, husky voice. 'Yes, I mean it.'

A prolonged, tense silence followed, and she felt his anger wash up against her like an energy field before he spoke. 'In that case, Jessica, you need have no fear that I shall touch you again.'

His voice was chilled, the words like icicles piercing her heart and freezing the blood in her veins. He walked away from her with purposeful, angry strides, and she watched him go with pain-filled eyes.

Sleep evaded her that night while her agonised mind replayed every incident from the moment the exotic rhythm of the *domba* drums had begun to pulsate through her veins. She had been like someone drugged; conscious only of her aching need for the love of a man who had no use for a woman except to inveigle her into an affair which he could end the moment he became bored with her.

God knew, she had tried right from the start to see him as a doctor, and not as a man, but she had found it quite impossible. Dane was not the kind of man one could ignore in the physical sense. He was too virile, too masculine, and her own words, spoken to her mother before her departure from Johannesburg, returned to taunt and mock her.

'When the right man comes along, the examination slab will be the farthest thing from my mind.'

That was the problem. Dane was not merely one of her fellow students, and neither was he a man to be observed only from a clinical point of view. His raw, virile masculinity had attacked her senses from their very first meeting, and although her extensive education had provided her with a first-class knowledge of the structure and function of the human body, it had left her ill-equipped to deal with the sensual side of it. All too soon she had found herself floundering in too deep waters, trying to cope with something which was far too strong for her, and loving him came much too easily, and much too swiftly.

The most dreadful part of it all was that she felt so ashamed. Not once during those moments while he had made love to her had he given her the slightest indication that he cared for her other than physically. If he had, she might not feel so ashamed now of her part in the encounter, but he had remained silent, and she could only come to the conclusion that she meant about as much to him as any other woman had meant to him before her.

He had been gentle in his passion, her heart told her, but her cynical mind contradicted that statement with. Of course he would be gentle. He's not the kind of man to use violence on a woman to get what he wanted.

'Oh, God!' Jessica moaned into the darkness. She was confused, and angry with herself more than with him, but it was not anger and confusion that brought a lump to her throat and tears to her eyes. It was a gnawing pain that refused to subside, and for the first time in many years she cried herself to sleep, but not even in her sleep did she escape the pain. Dane invaded her dreams in the most diabolical way. She was begging like a dog for the crumbs of his affection, but he laughed satanically while she squirmed beneath his rejection, and she finally awoke with a strangled cry on her lips to hear the birds singing in the trees outside the hut, while the early morning sun streamed in through the window.

She showered and dressed quickly, longing for a change of clothing which did not have the odour of wood smoke clinging to it to revive painful memories. The face that stared back at her in the mirror was hollow-eyed and pale, and she grimaced, adding an extra touch of lipstick to her lips before she picked up her medical bag and went along to see Chief Cedric.

CHAPTER NINE

DANE was in the hut with Chief Cedric when Jessica arrived, and a cool nod was the only recognition she received. Her queries were answered abruptly, but she did at least receive welcoming smiles from the Chief himself, and Sister Ravele. It eased that awful feeling that she was superfluous, and she remained quietly in the room while Dane carried out his examination.

There was no need for them to remain longer, for the Chief was out of danger, and could be left in Sister Ravele's capable hands. Jessica and Dane were persuaded to remain for breakfast, but before leaving the settlement they went to see Chief Cedric for the last time.

A great deal of noisy activity in the cattle enclosure near the Chief's hut drew their attention. The shouted commands of the herdsmen could be heard above the bellowing of the cattle, and a little distance away Patrick stood observing the proceedings critically. Jessica wondered what it was all in aid of, but she found out soon enough when they entered the Chief's hut.

'My brother has herded together a few of our best cattle,' Chief Cedric announced imperiously from his bed, and his black eyes were fixed intently on Dane. 'I want you to select ten cattle as payment for what you have done for me, and it is my wish that you find yourself a wife.'

This had amused Jessica the day before, but now it merely stirred up a fresh bout of pain. Dane did not seem to find it amusing either, for his tight-lipped expression remained unaltered.

'I appreciate your concern for my unmarried state,

Chief Cedric,' he replied with an edge to his politeness, 'but without sounding ungrateful, I know nothing about cattle and, when it comes to payment, I think it would be best if you discussed it with my partner, Dr O'Brien.'

The Chief made no comment, but an odd little smile hovered about his mouth before he clapped his hands to summon his head wife, and she came in as if she had been waiting outside the door for his signal. She carried in something which was wrapped up in a large piece of white tissue paper, and she departed swiftly when she had placed it into the Chief's hands. Lying in a reclining position did not seem to hamper the Chief at all, and Jessica could not deny her curiosity when he unwrapped the loosely folded tissue paper. What emerged was the beautifully cured skin of a python, and Jessica stared at it with a baffled expression on her face when he held it out towards her.

'The python is the god of fertility,' he explained when she had graciously accepted his gift. 'It will bring you children.'

Jessica felt her cheeks grow hot, and it was difficult enough maintaining her composure without Dane's glance sliding over her. 'I'm not married, Chief Cedric.'

'No matter,' he brushed aside her statement with that odd smile on his lips once again. 'A man is like a python when he is ready to seek his mate. His hunger is swift and strong when he uncoils, and when he strikes there is no escape.'

Jessica stared back at him in a bewildered fashion, but the only reply she received to her silent query was a tolerant smile.

'Go well, Dr Trafford, and you also, Dr Neal,' the Chief said, raising his right hand in an imperious farewell. 'My brother will drive you back to the airfield.'

'You were honoured,' Dane remarked casually when they were seated in the back of Patrick's long black limousine, and he gestured towards the gift she had received.

'A cured python skin isn't something they give away lightly.'

'I *am* honoured,' she assured him, fingering the skin lightly. 'But I'm also a little baffled by it.'

'The Venda are strange people with peculiar beliefs. They're also very intuitive people.'

His voice was lowered to exclude Patrick from their conversation, and she shot a quick, curious glance at Dane before she whispered, 'Are you trying to tell me that the Chief saw something in my future which I'm as yet unaware of?'

'Perhaps.'

Steel-grey eyes met hers, and the mockery in their depths made her lower her own glance uncomfortably. The memory of what had happened the night before was still too fresh, and too painfully humiliating. It would take time to come to terms with the fact that she had allowed Dane certain intimacies, and it was the memory of those intimacies that filled her with such horrifying shame.

Their flight back to Louisville was not as smooth as Jessica would have liked it. Clouds were gathering in the sky with a swiftness that hampered visibility, and it seemed as if the bushveld was going to receive the benefit of an early spring rain.

'What made you take up flying?' Dane interrupted her concentration on the dials before her.

'My brother took me for a flip once, and ever since then I was hooked.'

'Are there many more little surprises you have tucked away somewhere?'

'None that I can think of at the moment,' she smiled, relaxing her concentration slightly.

'You mentioned a brother,' Dane continued his probing queries.

'Gregory, yes.'

'Older or younger?'

'Older.' The Cessna bumped and swayed through an air pocket. 'He's an engineer.'

'That must have been a disappointment for your father.'

Jessica glanced at him quickly, but, to her surprise, there was no sign of mockery on his hard face.

'He was terribly disappointed at the time,' she said at length.

'But you made up for it.'

'In a way, yes.' Her lips curved in a reminiscent smile. 'My father had great plans for me to specialise in paediatrics.'

'And you didn't fancy the idea?'

'Not just yet.' The knife twisted in her heart. 'When my contract with Peter expires I might think of returning to my studies.'

Dane did not remark upon that, and his very silence filled her with intense despair. Whether she stayed on, or left, made no difference to him. He did not care beyond his immediate physical needs, and the knife jabbed deeper into her heart.

It started raining as they touched down on Mountain View's landing strip, and they were soaked to the skin during their dash from the hangar to where they had left their cars. The dark sky was ripped open by an electrifying crack of thunder, and flashes of lightning curled like tongues of fire through the heavy-laden clouds. The rain came down on to the parched earth with a vengeance, filling Jessica's nostrils with the fresh smell of damp soil as she leapt into her car, and the water was soon running like miniature rivers along every crack and crevice in the ground.

Bernard pulled up alongside them in his four-wheel-drive truck, indicating that he would follow them into town, and Jessica found this a comforting thought, for both she and Dane came close to needing Bernard's assistance on one occasion when their cars slithered across the road and threatened to become bogged down in the mud. It was a slow journey, with visibility virtually nil, but Bernard remained with them until they reached the outskirts of Louisville. The moment they were on the tarred road he saluted them by ramming his large fist on to the truck's horn, and returning his greeting in a similar fashion they watched him drive back the way they had come.

Jessica had never appreciated a shower and a change of clothing as much as she did that morning, and the storm had fortunately eased off by the time she reached the consulting-rooms where Peter O'Brien awaited them for news of Chief Cedric.

The flight to Venda had at last reminded Jessica of the medical she had to undergo for the renewal of her pilot's licence and, armed with the necessary forms, she approached Peter a few days later when they had a free half hour before going home to lunch.

'This shouldn't take long,' Peter smiled, picking up his pen.

The labouring engine of an approaching truck disturbed the midday silence, but neither of them paid much attention to it until it came to a squealing, shuddering halt outside the consulting-rooms. It was carrying a load of bellowing cattle, and they seemed intent upon trampling each other in the scorching heat of the sun, but the driver jumped down from the cab, apparently unconcerned about the misery of the protesting animals he was conveying.

'What on earth is all this?' Peter demanded sharply, and they rose simultaneously from their chairs to stare out of the window at the spectacle parked on their doorstep. 'What the devil is this truck-load of cattle doing here in the middle of town?'

A niggling suspicion was beginning to take shape in Jessica's mind, but she dared not voice it as she watched the white-clad figure marching out to confront the driver. 'Sister Hansen is sure to get rid of him quickly.'

'It doesn't look as though she's having much success,' Peter remarked wryly some minutes later. 'The driver is indicating to her that he intends remaining exactly where he is.'

'Perhaps we'd better go and find out what's going on,' Jessica suggested with a tentative curiosity, and Peter nodded abruptly.

'Having trouble, Sister Hansen?' he queried moments later when they joined her out on the pavement.

'I think Dr Trafford has a problem,' Emily Hansen replied dryly. 'This man implies that he's here with Chief Cedric Kapufu's blessings to deliver the promised cattle to Dr Trafford as payment for saving the Chief's life, and I've practically quoted him verbatim.'

'Is that so?' Peter murmured, his eyes dancing with mischief. 'Well, then, shouldn't we ask Dane to come out here?'

A smile creased Sister Hansen's round features. 'I'll do so at once, Dr O'Brien.'

Peter stared hard at the frothing, bellowing cattle, then he turned to Jessica. 'Do you know anything about this?'

'I'm afraid so, yes,' she replied, unable to restrain the laughter that tripped off her lips. 'The Chief wanted Dane to select the cattle personally, but Dane tried to evade the issue. Chief Cedric insisted that Dane was to buy himself a wife with the cattle.'

'Did he now?' Peter grinned humorously, but he sobered instantly when he glanced beyond her. 'Here is Dane.'

Dane, immaculate as always in an expensively tailored beige suit, gave the frustrated animals no more than a cursory glance before demanding abruptly, 'What's the problem?'

'No problem, Dane,' Peter replied smoothly, and Jessica had great difficulty in maintaining a sober expression when he added: 'I believe these cattle belong to you.'

'*What?*' Dane exploded, his eyes widening, then narrowing as comprehension dawned.

'Chief Cedric obviously considers that it's time you bought yourself a wife,' Peter pressed home the nature of this gift with a casualness which only barely concealed his amusement, and, for the first time since knowing Dane, Jessica saw him at a loss for words.

Their eyes met, and she realised, too late, that Dane did not need to be psychic to know where this last bit of information came from, and she looked away uncomfortably to where the truck driver had seated himself on the step of the cab. Unconcerned by their varied reactions, he was intent upon rolling himself a cigarette. He was carrying out the instructions of his revered Chief, and that was all that mattered to him.

'Shall we ask the driver to deliver the cattle to your home?' Peter queried calmly, breaking the strained, unnatural silence, but Dane rounded on him in something close to fury.

'You know damn well that I can't have these—these animals roaming about my garden!'

Visualising these skinny, sweating animals roaming through Dane's ornamental garden was too much for Jessica and, unable to control herself she burst out laughing.

'You could always send them along to your lady friend's parents in Pretoria,' she suggested daringly, trying to control herself, but finding it difficult when Peter and Emily Hansen were both trying to smother their laughter behind their hands.

'Dammit!' Dane exploded furiously, his eyes like blue slivers of ice slicing through Jessica. 'I don't *want* a wife, and when I do I won't need to buy her with cattle.'

'Well, you'll have to come to some decision about what you want done with them,' Peter reminded him as soon as he was able to subdue his laughter. 'It doesn't take an expert to come to the conclusion that these animals can't stay on that truck much longer.'

'Quite frankly, I don't care a fig in hell what happens to them!'

'You shouldn't look a gift horse in the mouth, Dane,' Jessica mocked him reprovingly, 'and you couldn't insult the Chief by not accepting his gift.'

Dane rounded on her with a look in his eyes that was instantly sobering. 'If you're so concerned, then why don't *you* do something about them.'

'It's the man who pays *lobola* for the woman of his choice, remember, and not the other way round,' she reminded him, smothering yet another bout of laughter.

'I have a suggestion,' Peter intervened, drawing Dane's ferocious attention away from Jessica. 'The driver could offload the cattle on the common at the show grounds, then I would ask Bernard to take them out to Mountain View for a while until you've decided what to do with them.'

'That's a very good suggestion,' Jessica giggled. 'But I can just imagine these miserable-looking animals parading about among Bernard's stud cattle.'

Peter rolled his eyes in mock horror, but his expression sobered suddenly as he faced Dane. 'I'll do my best to see to it that they're looked after for you.'

Dane thrust his clenched fists into the pockets of his pants and nodded abruptly. 'I'd appreciate that.'

'Sister Hansen,' Peter turned to the woman beside him, 'would you explain to this man in his own language how to get to the common while I get in touch with Bernard?'

'Certainly, Doctor,' Emily Hansen smiled, and marching across to where the driver sat smoking, she directed him towards the common at the show grounds with Dane looking on to confirm that he was in agreement with what was to be done with the cattle.

'Come along, Jessica,' Peter gestured her inside and out of the hot sun. 'When I've spoken to Bernard we'll get on with that medical of yours.'

While Peter used the telephone on Sister Hansen's desk, Jessica waited in his consulting-room. Five minutes passed, and still she waited. She decided eventually that Peter must be having difficulty in persuading Bernard to give Dane's cattle grazing, and she stifled a giggle. Ten minutes passed, and she was becoming restless when the door behind her opened and closed, and she swung round to face the man who had entered, but the smile on her lips froze when she found herself confronting Dane.

'What are you doing here?' she asked in a choked voice, her eyes on the hand that dipped into his pocket with something that looked suspiciously like a key, but she had to be mistaken, she told herself.

Dane walked round to the other side of the desk to scrutinise the forms lying on the blotter before he said casually, 'Peter received an urgent call from the hospital, and he asked me if I would do your medical for your pilot's licence.'

'He did what?' she demanded in a voice that squeaked with agitation, and she went hot and cold inside when Dane's icy gaze met hers.

'Take off your clothes.'

She stared at him in something close to horror. 'I beg your pardon?'

'I said take off your clothes.'

'You must be mad!' she gasped, her eyes dark and stormy, and her heart pounding out a frightened tattoo against her ribs. 'There's no necessity for me to do that!'

'When I examine someone I make a thorough job of it,' Dane replied coldly, the line of his jaw as hard and unrelenting as the wall behind him. 'Take off your clothes.'

Panic rose within her to mingle with her anger. 'I'm damned if I will!'

There was a frightening little silence as their glances clashed, and the look in those cold grey eyes sent a shiver of apprehension through her long before he stepped round the desk and advanced towards her purposefully.

'Are you going to take them off yourself, or do I have to take them off for you?' His smile was the smile of the devil himself. 'It wouldn't be the first time I've undressed you, would it?'

She backed away from him towards the door with jerky movements, her hands against her flaming cheeks. 'If you so much as touch me I'll scream,' she hissed through her teeth.

'Scream all you want,' he drawled lazily, but his smile was cold now, and infinitely dangerous. 'Sister Hansen has gone off to lunch, and that door is locked, by the way.'

Her hands fell limply to her sides, and the colour drained from her cheeks to leave her deathly pale. 'You fiend!'

'Don't be tedious, Jessica,' he sighed harshly. 'Take off your clothes, and let's get on with the examination.'

She had never been afraid of Dane before, but she was afraid now, and the saliva dried up in her mouth when his cold eyes travelled over her with systematic slowness, stripping her mentally down to her skin until she actually felt as if she were standing naked before him. The blood surged painfully back into her cheeks, and she shrank from him inwardly even as she suspected the reason for his behaviour.

'All right, Dane, you've had your fun,' she managed huskily, passing the tip of her tongue over her dry lips, and totally unaware of the provocativeness of her action.

'It was unforgivable of me to laugh at your discomfort because the Chief has this silly notion that you need a wife, and I admit that I told Peter about it. That was wrong of me, and now you're getting back at me in this way, but I think it's time we call it quits, don't you?'

'It seems as though you actually want me to undress you,' he remarked coldly, ignoring the plea in her voice, but, when he advanced towards her, her hand rose from her side of its own volition to strike him a stinging blow across his lean, hard cheek.

Horrified by her own actions, she stared up into eyes which had become narrowed to angry slits. She tried to speak, but no sound seemed to pass her lips. She had done something totally unforgivable, but, heaven knew, she had not meant to. She had been driven to it by fear, but she doubted whether Dane would understand this in his present mood.

'I swore that I'd never touch you again, but I'm damned if I'll let you get away with that,' he ground out the words, then punishing fingers gripped her wrists and she was jerked up against him.

Her arms were twisted behind her back until they ached with the pressure he put on them, and her breasts hurt against the hardness of his chest, but this was nothing compared to the brutal savagery of his kiss. Her lips were crushed against her teeth until she tasted the saltiness of her own blood in her mouth, and her head was forced back to such an extent that she feared her neck would snap. Her cry of agony was no more than a whimpering sound deep down in her throat, but it seemed to bring Dane to his senses, and he released her so abruptly that she staggered back against the instrument cabinet in a dazed fashion.

'You may go,' he said in a clipped voice, unlocking the door and opening it wide with surprisingly controlled movements which she envied while she stood there shaking like a leaf with her breath coming jerkily over parted, swollen lips. 'As you said, we're quits.'

Tears sprang to her eyes, but fortunately he did not see them. He was standing with his back turned towards her, staring out of the window with his clenched fists resting on the windowsill, and she did not wait for a second invitation to escape.

In the privacy of her bathroom at the cottage, she examined her lips in the mirror above the basin. They looked bruised, and slightly swollen, and on the inside of her top lip she could see distinctly where her teeth had pierced the flesh. It would heal within a day or two, but the bruises on her wrists would take a little longer.

It was strange, she thought, brushing away the tears which threatened to overflow once more. She had credited Dane with a sense of humour, and she had seen flashes of it during the past months, but for some reason it must have deserted him entirely on this occasion.

'Damn!' she muttered to herself, holding a cold, damp cloth to her lips. 'He didn't have to behave in such a beastly manner!'

She sat down heavily on the edge of the bath and tried to view the entire episode sensibly. Dane did not take kindly to being laughed at, and she could almost understand his desire to vent his anger on her. Perhaps, if she had taken his retaliation, nothing untoward would have happened, but she had allowed herself to become frightened, and she had reacted instinctively by striking him.

That had been her second and final mistake, and when she considered it in that light she supposed that she had got off lightly. Dane was not the kind of man who would tolerate that sort of treatment from a woman, and even though her impulsive action had been motivated by fear, it was not something he would take without a murmur.

Jessica sighed and flung the cloth into the basin. She owed Dane an apology, and it was not going to be easy.

'Jessica . . .' Peter entered her consulting-room late that afternoon, waving a form at her. 'About this medical of yours . . .'

'Why in heaven's name did you ask Dane to do it?' she demanded before he could continue.

'I never did anything of the kind,' Peter denied at once. 'I asked him to tell you that I was called away to the hospital, and that I'd do your medical later this afternoon.'

'I see,' she murmured, her annoyance evaporating swiftly.

'He played a trick on you, did he?' Peter questioned, his blue eyes dancing with mischief, and Jessica nodded slowly.

'I don't think he enjoyed being laughed at, and he tried to get his own back on me.'

'Did he succeed?'

Without actually realising what she was doing, she ran a tentative finger across her lips and smiled ruefully. 'Have you ever known him to fail?'

When Peter left her room ten minutes later, leaving the completed form on her desk, she scraped together her flagging courage and went along to Dane's rooms. He was shrugging himself into his jacket when she entered, and it was only when he turned that he saw her standing just inside the door.

His eyebrows rose sharply. 'Was there something you wanted?'

'I owe you an apology, Dane,' she said quickly before she lost her nerve, and there was a flicker of surprise in the eyes appraising her so coolly.

'Are you apologising for not undressing when I asked you to?'

Her anger flared at his mockery. 'You know very well that I'm referring to the fact that I struck you.'

'Don't be silly, Jessica,' he countered abruptly. 'You

know damn well you enjoyed it.'

Something tightened in her chest. 'Did you enjoy the punishment you dished out?'

'At the time, yes.' His eyes flicked over her small, slender frame, and lingered finally on her bruised lips. 'You deserved it, but right now you deserve something better.'

Before she had time to realise his intentions, he had closed the door and she was a prisoner in his arms. Resistance was a fleeting thought that fluttered and died the moment his lips met hers, and this time there was no brutality in his kiss. His lips teased and caressed, awakening a throbbing response within her, but when his hand clasped her breast through the silk of her blouse, she came to her senses and struggled against him.

'No . . . don't . . .' she managed, her breath coming fast over her parted lips, and she was released at once.

Dane's expression hardened. 'What are you afraid of this time, Jessica? Yourself?'

He had picked up his bag and was striding from the room before she could think of anything to say, and what *could* she have said, she wondered afterwards. Contrary to what she had imagined, Dane had known of the fear he had instilled in her earlier that day, but she dared not let him suspect to what extent she feared her own emotions— the humiliation would be too much to bear.

Two weeks later Jessica's parents arrived to spend the weekend with her, and they brought with them the adoption papers which Peter and Vivien had to sign at the local magistrate's offices. Jonathan Neal had somehow managed the impossible, and a laborious, usually lengthy procedure had been shortened miraculously.

A *braai* was arranged at the O'Brien home on the Saturday evening to celebrate the occasion, and Jessica counted close on thirty people seated around the barbecue in the well-lit, spacious garden. Other than the O'Briens and Jessica's parents, there were familiar faces such as Oom Hennie and Tante Maria Delport, and Bernard and Olivia King, but the rest of the guests were virtually strangers to Jessica.

She was sitting with Olivia's chubby little baby on her lap when Dane arrived, but Peter spared her the task of introducing him to her parents, and she could not help noticing how her mother seemed to melt beneath Dane's charm.

When the mouthwatering aroma of meat roasting on the open fires permeated the air, Peter drew Vivien and Megan to his side, and commanded everyone's attention.

'I'd like to propose a toast,' he announced, placing a hand on Megan's shoulder and raising his glass. 'To our daughter, Megan Leigh O'Brien. I'd like her to know how happy we are to be able to call her our own, and we want to share our happiness with all of you.'

'To Megan,' everyone chorussed loudly, and happily, raising their glasses to their lips, and Jessica could not help thinking that she had never seen three happier people than Peter, Vivien and Megan.

'There is one other thing,' Peter's voice rose above the excited chatter of the well-wishes. 'I'd like to drink a toast to Jessica Neal for bringing Megan into our lives.'

'To Jessica,' the voices of the guests rose in unison, and Jessica felt her cheeks grow warm with everyone's attention riveted on her.

Across the garden Dane's eyes met hers, and although she could not read his expression she was certain that it could only be mockery curving his mouth as he raised his glass to her and swallowed down the remainder of his drink.

Jessica looked away, a frown of annoyance on her brow and, when the excitement finally died down, Tante Maria leaned across Olivia to say, 'It's time you found yourself a husband, *kindjie*. You would look lovely with a child of your own in your arms.'

'Tante Maria's right,' Olivia teased. 'You're incredibly good with children and you shouldn't waste too much time settling down and having a few of your own.'

Jessica hid her pain successfully behind a smile. 'I have to find the right husband first.'

'What about Dane?' Tante Maria persisted wickedly. 'I've always said that he's good husband material.'

Olivia, with the advantage over Tante Maria in the sense that she knew Jessica better, guessed that something was amiss, and she cast a reproving glance in the older woman's direction.

'We're wrong to tease, Tante Maria,' she said firmly. 'Jessica will find the right man in good time.'

Tante Maria accepted this with a silent nod, oblivious of the look that passed between the two younger women. Olivia had somehow sensed Jessica's unhappiness, and Jessica was eternally grateful to her for her remarkable understanding.

'I think you'd better take Logan,' Jessica said at length, placing the wriggling child in Olivia's arms. 'I'd like to have a few words with Megan.'

Jessica strolled to where she had seen Megan and Frances only moments before. Dane was standing among the men who were grouped around the fires, his broad back turned towards her, and his head tilted slightly at a listening angle while Bernard spoke to him. He looked relaxed without his jacket, and his shirt sleeves were rolled up to above his elbows, but even at that distance she sensed an alertness, a flexing of the muscles as if in preparation for action, and everything within her seemed to reach out to him with a longing so intense that the breath stilled in her throat. He turned suddenly, almost as if he had known she was there, and his compelling glance captured hers, holding it for a few heart-stopping seconds before she managed to free herself and continue her search for the children.

'Hello there, you two,' she said moments later, interrupting their imaginative exploration among the trees and shrubs, and placing an arm about each of them, she asked, 'How does it feel to be Megan Leigh O'Brien?'

'I'm so happy, Dr Jessica.' Wide blue eyes gazed up at Jessica, and in the light of the distant fires she could not miss the happiness and contentment lurking there. 'Now I know that I never have to leave here again.'

Jessica glanced down at the long-limbed, dark-haired daughter of Bernard King. 'How do you feel about it, Frances?'

White teeth flashed in a wide smile. 'It's super having a cousin, and during the December holidays I'm going to teach her how to ride a horse.'

'That would be nice,' Jessica agreed, hugging them both.

'I can't wait!' Megan announced, bouncing excitedly beside Jessica.

'What can't you wait for, young Megan?' Dane's deep voice asked directly behind Jessica, and it took every ounce of will-power to maintain her outwardly calm appearance as she released the children and turned to face him.

'Frances is going to teach me how to ride a horse,' Megan explained, smiling up at Dane in an easy, unrestrained manner which Jessica envied at that moment.

'Do you ride well, Frances?' Dane turned his attention to the more reserved of the two children.

'Yes, I do,' Frances replied at once. 'My father taught me, and he's an excellent horseman.'

'Do you ride, Doctor Jessica?' Megan wanted to know, and Jessica shook her head.

'I'm afraid not.'

'Olivia can't ride either, but my father says that if you're nervous of horses then it's best to stay away from them,' Frances intervened knowingly. 'Animals are ultra-sensitive, you see.'

'There are humans who are equally ultra-sensitive,' Dane remarked drily, and Jessica felt his mocking gaze resting on her when he added softly, 'I can think of one in particular who shies away from reality like a frightened filly.'

His bare forearm brushed against hers, sending a spark of awareness shooting throughout her entire body, and she stepped away from him jerkily.

'If you'll excuse me,' she said abruptly, glancing beyond him with a measure of relief, 'I think Vivien wants to have a word with me.'

Her excuse to escape his subtle reference to herself was valid, but nevertheless she felt his mocking eyes following her as she crossed the garden to where Vivien awaited her.

'I've been wanting a private word with you ever since your father arrived here yesterday with the adoption papers,' said Vivien, drawing Jessica a little aside from the laughter and activity around the fires. 'We have you to thank for this, Jessica, and I don't really know where to begin.'

'Don't say anything, Vivien,' Jessica interrupted hastily. 'Just be happy.'

'Oh, we are!' Vivien sighed, a suspicious-looking moisture filling her dark eyes as she gripped Jessica's hands. 'Tremendously happy.'

'Then that's enough for me,' Jessica assured her gently.

'Talking of happiness,' Vivien laughed a little shakily, brushing her tears away unobtrusively, 'Dane doesn't look too happy these days. Do you think he's having problems with that woman of his in Pretoria?'

Jessica stiffened, refusing to let her glance follow the direction Vivien's had taken. 'I really wouldn't know.'

'It wouldn't surprise me if he's fallen in love at last,'

Vivien laughed. 'He has that look about him, and it would serve him right if that Summers woman turns him down flat.'

Jessica found herself murmuring something appropriate, but she felt raw inside. Was Dane still seeing Sylvia Summers? She tried to tell herself that it was none of her business, but the question gnawed away at her until she felt like screaming.

For the remainder of the evening Jessica avoided Dane as much as was humanly possible, but she could not avoid noticing that he spent a considerable amount of time in the company of her parents. They liked him, she could see that, and she was aware of her mother's curious, enquiring glances when she refused to respond to her mother's silent entreaty to join them.

CHAPTER TEN

'NICE chap, that Dane Trafford,' Jonathan Neal remarked that night when they had returned to Jessica's cottage after the *braai*. 'And he's clever too.'

'I found him utterly charming,' Amelia added enthusiastically, then she eyed her daughter thoughtfully. 'By the way, Jessica, I invited him to join us for dinner tomorrow evening.'

'Oh, Mother!' Jessica sighed exasperatedly.

'Well, why not?' Amelia demanded indignantly.

'Did he accept?'

'He said he would be delighted.' Jessica groaned inwardly at her mother's reply, and some of her displeasure must have shown on her face, for Amelia turned on her at once. 'Really, Jessica, I can't see what you could possibly have against him. He's charming, good-looking, and much too masculine for you to put him on that mental slab of yours. No woman, not even you, Jessica, could look at him without something totally unclinical stirring in your breast.'

Jessica would have found her mother's remark amusing at one time, but the amusing side of it escaped her at that moment. 'You're right, Mother. He's all the things you say, but——'

'But what?' her mother prompted.

'We don't get along so well, that's all,' she added lamely, biting down hard on her lip.

'But why not, for heaven's sake?'

'Perhaps it's a chemical reaction,' her father intervened irritably. 'Put two chemicals together, and they either repulse each other, or they set off a responsive spark.'

Amelia glanced sharply at her husband. 'I've always disliked your chemical theories, Jonathan, but on this occasion it makes sense.' Now it was Jessica's turn to encounter the sharpness of her mother's glance. 'Which is it, Jessica? Do you and Dane Trafford repulse each other, or is there a responsive spark, as your father puts it?'

'Leave this inquisition, Amelia,' Jonathan grunted, correctly interpreting the silent entreaty in his daughter's glance. 'It's late, and we're all tired.'

Amelia opened her mouth to say something, but Jessica leapt in first with a quick 'goodnight' before she escaped to her own room.

She slept very badly that night, and she was in a waspish mood on the Sunday at the prospect of Dane's visit that evening. It absolutely grated her to listen to her mother humming merrily to herself while she planned the evening meal, but, against her will, she finally became inveigled into the preparations.

They were in the kitchen that evening, putting the finishing touches to the salads, when there was a sharp knock on the front door.

'That will be Dane,' Amelia said excitedly, wiping her fluttering hands on her apron, and eyeing Jessica expectantly.

'Probably,' she agreed, shrugging carelessly.

'Well, aren't you going to let him in?' Amelia persisted hopefully.

'Daddy's in the lounge, so I presume he'll let Dane in.'

'Well, really!' Amelia exclaimed indignantly. 'You could at least go in there and say good evening.'

'You invited him, Mother,' Jessica replied tritely. 'You go in and say good evening.'

Amelia Neal shook her head, unable to fathom the workings of her daughter's mind as Jonathan's voice reached their ears.

'Come in, Dane,' he said pleasantly. 'Come in.'

'I hope I'm not too early,' Dane's deep voice contained a hint of apology.

'Not at all,' Jonathan assured him. 'The women are in the kitchen, and I dislike drinking alone.'

There was a brief silence during which Jonathan obviously took Dane into the lounge, and it was during this silence that Amelia removed the apron about her waist, then she glared at her daughter and said reprovingly, 'Well, if you've forgotten your manners, Jessica, then I certainly haven't forgotten mine.'

Left alone in the kitchen, Jessica tried to prepare herself in some way for her meeting with Dane, but it was difficult concentrating on what she was doing when every particle of her being was concentrated on what was happening in the lounge. She heard the clink of glasses, and the murmur of voices, and she wished suddenly that this night was at an end.

She was adding a decorative slip of parsley to a bowl of salad when Dane walked into the kitchen, and he instantly dwarfed it with his size.

'I believe you'll have a sherry,' he said calmly, extending a glass towards her.

'Thank you,' she murmured, almost spilling some of the liquid when his fingers brushed against her own.

She took a sip of sherry to steady her nerves while his cool, assessing glance travelled over her, and she knew that nothing missed those razor-sharp eyes; not the trembling of her hand, nor her displeasure at his presence.

'I gather you don't like the idea that I was invited for dinner.'

'You gather correctly,' she said, realising that there was no point in denying how she felt.

'Why?' he shot the question at her.

'We work together, but I see no reason why we should mix socially as well.'

His perfectly chiselled mouth tightened into a harsh,

thin line. 'You don't believe in beating about the bush, do you?'

'I could say the same for you,' she said coldly, her challenging glance meeting his, and she saw that familiar gleam of mockery leap into his eyes.

'That's right,' he said. 'I believe in speaking my mind, and right this minute I'd give anything to have you alone to myself in one of Chief Cedric's guest huts.' His cold-blooded reference to those moments of intimacy they had shared sent a heated wave of anger and humiliation surging into her cheeks, and her hands clenched the bowl before her as she experienced the desire to throw something at him, but he seemed to read her mind in that diabolical way of his. 'Don't ruin a perfectly good salad, Jessica,' he warned quietly.

'I think it's despicable of you to remind me of that night,' she said in a voice that was husky with the effort to control her anger, and she turned from him to hide the tears of frustration and despair which began to hover on her lashes.

'I've never denied that I'm a despicable character, but you can't say that I've ever left you in doubt as to what's on my mind.'

There was some truth in that, she had to admit to herself as she felt him come up behind her, and the touch of his hands on her shoulders was a sweet agony she longed to surrender to, but she knew that she dared not.

'If you don't mind, Dane, I——'

'A truce?' he interrupted with an unexpected suggestion, turning her to face him, but she kept her eyes lowered to the hand he extended towards her. 'We'll call a truce for tonight only, if you like, and tomorrow I'll give you permission to call me all the names you may care to.'

Jessica hesitated, wary of his suggestion, then she placed her hand in his. 'Very well,' she sighed, 'but please understand that I'm only doing this for my parents' sake.'

'I understand perfectly,' Dane assured her with that familiar hint of mockery in his voice, and when his fingers tightened about hers she knew that it had been a mistake giving him her hand, for he had no intention of releasing it as quickly as she would have wished. 'You have such small, beautifully shaped hands, Jessica.'

He turned her hand palm upwards into his left hand, and with the fingers of his right hand he traced the lines across her palm. There was something so sensually erotic in what he was doing that her pulses leapt in a wild response, and a familiar yearning surged through her until her limbs trembled.

'Don't do that!' she managed at last, her voice a hoarse whisper as she jerked her hand free and stepped away from him.

'My apologies,' he bowed cynically. 'Bring your sherry with you, and join us in the lounge for a few minutes.'

'It will have to be a very short few minutes,' she agreed, regaining her composure with an effort. 'The dinner will spoil if it's left too long.'

The rest of the evening passed somehow without a hitch. Dane's interest in neuro-surgery gave him and her father a great deal in common to talk about, but Dane was tactful enough not to linger too long on the subject for her mother's sake. He was a perfect guest to the very last detail, and neither did he outstay his welcome, for it was not yet ten o'clock when he announced that it was time for him to leave. Amelia, naturally, tried to persuade him to remain longer, but Dane was adamant.

'It's still reasonably early, I admit,' he said, 'but you have a long journey ahead of you tomorrow.'

Amelia agreed with him reluctantly, and a few minutes later Jessica somehow found herself accompanying Dane out to his car.

A tense silence seemed to settle between them, and she wondered why. They had managed to behave pleasantly enough towards each other in the company of her parents, but quite suddenly there seemed to be nothing to say.

In the darkness beside his Mustang, he took her hands in his, and something in the way he said, 'Goodnight,' sent a warning flashing through her mind. The truce was over, she realised, and pulling her hands free of his, she stepped away from him, breathing a little easier with a reasonable distance between them.

'Goodnight, Dane,' she said with rigid politeness, watching him slide behind the wheel of his car, but before he drove away she heard his soft, mocking laughter, and it drifted towards her on the scented night air to hover about her as she watched his car disappear down the street.

'I thought you said you didn't get along with Dane?' her mother demanded accusingly when she joined them in the lounge moments later.

'We do get along sometimes, but not always,' Jessica replied cautiously.

'I think he's an extremely nice man. Don't you, Jonathan?'

'Nice isn't quite the adjective I would use to describe Dane, Amelia,' he replied, grinning as he clenched his pipe between his teeth.

'How would you describe him, then?'

'Oh, I don't know,' Jonathan shrugged. 'I've never been good with words, you know that.'

'What about above-average intelligence with just the right touch of arrogance to get what he wants out of life?' Jessica intervened.

Her father raised his eyebrows a fraction. 'I sense a touch of animosity there, but I would say you've described him perfectly. He's certainly extremely intelligent, and a man needs a certain amount of arrogance to cope with life.'

'You're probably right,' Jessica sighed.

'I hope you'll invite him over next time we're here?' Amelia said, her eyes intent upon Jessica.

'If you like him that much, then I'll make a point of it,' Jessica replied with a cynical smile curving her mouth.

'I really don't understand you,' Amelia sighed exasperatedly. 'Dane Trafford is the most magnificent specimen of manhood I've seen in a long time.'

'I agree with you.'

'Well then?' Amelia demanded expectantly.

'Well then, what?' Jessica questioned evasively.

'Why don't you do something about it?'

Jessica eyed her mother contemplatively with a hint of mischief in her dark brown eyes. 'Are you encouraging me to have an affair with him?'

'Certainly not!' her mother exclaimed in a shocked voice.

'Well, that's all Dane Trafford is interested in,' Jessica said, the mischief in her eyes replaced by bitterness.

'No man is interested in marriage until the right woman makes it her business to see to it that he is,' Amelia persisted.

'What makes you think that I'm the right woman to make Dane interested in marriage, and who says I'm interested enough to try?' Jessica returned swiftly.

'Stalemate,' Jonathan observed drily, rising tiredly from his chair. 'I'm going to bed.'

'Wait for me, Jonathan,' Amelia said quickly and, getting to her feet, she shook her head at her daughter. 'I really wish I understood you, Jessica.'

Jessica was too busy during the following week to see much of Dane, and most of her evenings were spent at the hospital, or at home trying to catch up on a few hours of sleep.

She arrived home a little late from the consulting-rooms

on the Friday afternoon, hoping for at least one peaceful night in this long, tiring week, but her hopes began to dwindle when she saw a strange car parked in the street outside the cottage. The woman who climbed out of the car was also a stranger to Jessica. Tall, fair, and possessing an unmistakable elegance, she finally approached Jessica, and she was undoubtedly one of the most beautiful women Jessica had ever seen.

'Dr Neal?'

The voice was musical, the feline purr faintly familiar, and a frown settled on Jessica's brow as she nodded slowly. 'That's right.'

'I was hoping to see you.' Grey-green eyes travelled over Jessica, carrying out a critical inspection which was totally confusing until she said: 'I'm Sylvia Summers.'

'Oh!'

Coral-pink lips parted in a smile to reveal small, perfectly even teeth, but the smile did not reach the cat-like eyes. 'I can see you've heard of me.'

'I believe Dr Trafford has mentioned you, yes,' Jessica replied with care, her calm outward appearance giving no indication of her bewildered and slightly confused feelings at that moment. 'Won't you come in?'

'Thank you,' Sylvia smiled, accepting Jessica's invitation graciously, and Jessica unlocked the door, standing aside to allow Sylvia to procede her into the cottage.

Seated in her lounge, Jessica realised that one would have to be blind not to realise what Dane had seen in this woman. She was sophisticated, beautiful, and extremely feminine, and the latter was something which would appeal to someone with a virile masculinity such as Dane's.

'What can I do for you, Miss Summers?' Jessica asked politely when an awkward silence threatened.

'It's not what you can do for me, but more likely what I can do for you,' Sylvia replied, crossing one shapely leg over the other. 'What I have to say to you is by nature of a warning.'

Jessica stiffened in protest. 'Miss Summers, I think you've made a——'

'Don't misunderstand me,' Sylvia interrupted smoothly. 'I'm not here as the jealous mistress who intends scratching your eyes out for meddling with what I considered my property. I'm here to warn you that if you think Dane is going to marry you, then you're mistaken. He doesn't operate that way. And if you think that by becoming his mistress you could hold him to you in some way, then forget it. You'll last a year, maybe two, then he'll give you your walking ticket, and tell you to scat.' There was something malicious in her smile now. 'That's Dane Trafford, and it will take someone mighty special to put the chains on him.'

Jessica did not need to be told that she could never be that someone, and even though she had known this from the very beginning, it somehow still had the power to hurt her.

'May I know who or what led you to believe that there could possibly be anything between Dane and myself?' Jessica heard herself ask in a cool, detached voice.

'Dane told me,' came the smooth reply, and that coral-pink mouth twisted with bitterness. 'You should know by now that Dane isn't one to mince his words. When he wants to end a relationship he says so, and then tells you why.'

Jessica could not quite believe that she had heard correctly. 'Dane told you that there was—something between us?'

'No,' Sylvia smiled thinly. 'His exact words were, "I want her, and I'm going to get her", so be warned. He's set his sights on you, and if you don't duck you're going to get it right where it hurts most.' She rose elegantly to her feet, and Jessica followed suit a little more jerkily to withstand the intense scrutiny of this woman's critical glance as it swept over her. 'Funny . . .' Sylvia smiled coldly, 'I would have said that you weren't his type at all.'

The silence was broken by the sound of tyres crunching on the gravel outside, and then footsteps could be heard approaching the cottage. Jessica stiffened. She knew the identity of her caller, and so, apparently, did Sylvia, judging by the odd expression that flitted across her beautiful face.

The door was flung open and Dane filled the lounge with his awesome presence. He was still wearing the dark grey suit he had worn that day, but he had removed his tie, and the top buttons of his shirt were undone, giving Jessica a glimpse of his tanned, hair-roughened chest.

Cool grey eyes met Jessica's briefly, then he glanced at Sylvia, and his voice possessed that icy chill of winter as he said: 'I thought you were on your way back to Pretoria.'

'As a matter of fact, darling, I'm just leaving,' Sylvia laughed easily, and with a careless wave of a perfectly manicured hand, she added: 'Have fun!'

She swept past Jessica and Dane, her heavy perfume lingering in the air between them like an impregnable barrier long after she had driven away.

'I had an idea she'd come here,' Dane's harsh voice sliced through the incredibly tense silence. 'What did she tell you?' he demanded, but Jessica was in no mood for a post-mortem of her enlightening conversation with Sylvia Summers.

'She told me nothing that I don't already know,' she snapped.

'That leaves a lot to the imagination, so you'd better tell me,' he insisted with biting cynicism.

'You don't need to be enlightened as far as your character is concerned, but I'll tell you what I think of you,' she rounded on him in a blinding fury. 'You're a cruel, callous brute, and all I can feel for you at this moment is contempt!'

His mouth tightened and his expression darkened with ominous fury. 'So it's contempt you feel for me, is it?'

He was like a sleek, black leopard, his muscles tensed and ready for the kill. Jessica prepared herself for the inevitable, but it never came. The shrill, persistent ring of the telephone intervened, jarring her tortured nerves, and she turned from Dane during that brief moment of respite to answer it.

'Dr Neal speaking,' she said into the mouthpiece, hoping the caller would not notice the slight tremor in her voice, but the girl on the hospital switchboard was fortunately too intent upon the urgency of her call. Jessica gathered her scattered wits about her to listen intently to what the girl was saying, and moments later she replaced the receiver with an abrupt, 'I'll come at once.'

When she turned round she discovered that she was alone, and neither was Dane's car outside when she reversed her Alfa into the street. She had never seen him in such a fury before, and she shivered at the thought of what might have happened had the telephone not interrupted at that precise moment. Her own anger had been more than enough for her to cope with at that moment, but the hurt was something else. Sylvia Summers had told her nothing she had not known before, this much was true, but she had somehow axed every scrap of hope Jessica had still been foolish enough to nurture.

There was no time to think of herself during the next few hours. She had a difficult confinement on her hands, and it was well after eleven that night before the baby was born. Jessica had to deliver him with instruments, and although the mother was exhausted, the infant was none the worse for the delay.

'You look a bit peckish, Doctor,' the night Sister on duty remarked when Jessica had changed out of her theatre clothes. 'Have you had anything to eat yet this evening?'

'There hasn't been time,' Jessica smiled ruefully, aware of that hollow feeling at the pit of her stomach.

'I thought not,' the Sister nodded and, ushering Jessica into her small office, she ordered tea and sandwiches from the canteen, and left Jessica alone for a few minutes.

Jessica slumped into a vacant chair, too tired to object. Her limbs felt like lead, but her mind was in a chaotic mess. Thoughts came and went with frantic precision like painful darts aimed at her very soul. Her image was reflected in the glass cabinet against the wall, and she looked small, drab, and pathetic. Her shoulders sagged with weariness and, in comparison with Sylvia's elegant beauty, she looked about as interesting as the faded, rather tatty paper flower in the empty peanut butter jar on the desk. Seeing herself as she was at that moment, she knew that she never did and never would stand a chance to win Dane's love. 'It would take someone mighty special to put the chains on him,' Sylvia had said, and Jessica felt as if she were dying slowly inside with the agony of despair.

The refreshments arrived, but Jessica was barely conscious of drinking her tea, let alone eating the sandwiches, although she did feel a little less hollow on the inside a half hour later.

'I hope, for your sake, Doctor, that there'll be no further calls tonight,' the Sister announced pleasantly when Jessica finally wished her goodnight with a tired smile.

Jessica was physically and mentally exhausted when she arrived back at her cottage. It was after midnight, and all she wanted at that moment was to crawl into her bed to sleep away the rest of that disturbing night. Everything else could wait until tomorrow, she decided as she turned the key in the lock and pushed open the door.

'Jessica?' Dane's voice, coming out of the darkness

behind her, jarred her sensitive nerves with such violence that a choked cry escaped her, and she swung round sharply to see him disengage himself from the shadows of the bougainvillaea ranking on the pergola. He looked so tall, so dark, and so devastatingly attractive that fear, excitement and longing clamoured simultaneously through her veins to leave her leaning weakly against the door frame as she watched him walk towards her. 'I'm sorry if I startled you,' he surprised her with an apology.

She stared up into those unfathomable grey eyes when he stepped into the square of light coming from the lounge, and a frown creased her brow. 'What are you doing here at this time of night?'

'I had to talk to you.'

'Couldn't it have waited until the morning?'

His jaw was set in a hard, unrelenting line. 'What I have to say can't wait.'

'I suppose you'd better come in, then,' she sighed at length, knowing only too well that it would be futile to argue with him, and she led the way inside. She felt incredibly tense and nervous as she dumped her bag on the nearest chair and pushed a tired hand through her already touselled curls. 'Coffee?' she asked abruptly out of mere politeness.

'Later, perhaps,' he declined, discarding his jacket and turning to face her. 'Jessica, I'd like to explain.'

'Explain?' she laughed with forced casualness, gathering her scattered wits about her to do battle with him. 'Good heavens, Dane, I can't think of anything that needs explaining.'

'I have an idea that Sylvia never told you the entire truth.'

'She didn't have to spell it out for me, Dane,' she told him tiredly, turning away from the fatal attraction he had for her. 'You told me quite some time ago that you wanted me, and Sylvia merely underlined the fact that you were planning to intensify your efforts to lure me into an affair.'

'Is that all she told you?' he laughed, and his laughter ignited her dormant fury.

'For God's sake, Dane!' she exclaimed, swinging round to face him once more, and her eyes were dark pools of pain in her white, pinched face. 'Do you need me to repeat verbatim everything she told me?'

'It would make it a lot easier for me if I knew exactly what I'm supposed to have said to her.'

'Oh, very well,' Jessica sighed, willing to do anything at that moment if it would get rid of him. 'With regard to myself, you were supposed to have said; and I quote—"I want her, and I'm going to get her"—unquote, and I can tell you right now, Dane, that you're not going to succeed. You have a misguided idea that you can pick up and discard women in much the same manner you do your clothes, but I won't be picked up and dropped at your pleasure.'

'Jessica . . .'

'Don't touch me!' she cried hoarsely, moving jerkily out of his reach. 'I think you're the most insensitive man I've ever had the misfortune to meet, and if you don't mind I'd like you to leave now.'

Cold fury suddenly etched his lean features. 'I'm damned if I'll leave before I've had my say!'

'Nothing you may say could be of any possible interest to me.'

Dane was again that sleek, black jungle cat leaping into action, and this time there was no escape. Her arms were pinned ruthlessly at her sides as he crushed her against the hard length of his body, and she could only stare up into the glittering fury of his eyes with a helplessness that made her want to weep.

'If it isn't words you want, Jessica, then perhaps you'll settle for this,' his voice lashed her before his mouth claimed hers with a savagery she had known once before.

She tried to struggle free, but her puny efforts were futile, and the punishment continued until, exhausted, she went limp against him, surrendering herself to the primitive emotions aroused by his savage kiss. Dane did not spare her, not even when her lips parted in an unwilling response. Tears filled her eyes and spilled from beneath her lashes, but it was only when a sob rose in her throat that he released her.

'Will you listen to me now?' he demanded harshly as she stood shaken and trembling before him.

'I hate you, Dane Trafford!' she cried huskily, her vision distorted through a film of tears. 'I hate you, do you hear me?'

'Will you marry me, Jessica?'

She sucked her breath in sharply, and a fresh bout of fury shook through her. 'Are you crazy? You know damn well that you're offering me marriage for the simple reason that you know you can't get me any other way.'

'I don't want you any other way.'

She dashed the tears from her eyes with an impatient hand, and stared up at him, wanting desperately to believe him, but not a flicker of emotion crossed his granite-hard features. There was nothing there to give her any indication as to his feelings, no tenderness in his eyes, no softening of the hard, often cruel mouth, and she clamped down firmly on that rising tide of hope.

'You don't mean that, Dane. You're only saying so because you think it might act as a persuasive. Oh, you're very clever, I'll grant you that,' she laughed bitterly. 'You know just how to bait the hook, but I'm not going to bite.'

'Dammit, Jessica!' He slammed his fist into the palm of his left hand as if he wished she were the recipient, and she flinched nervously. 'Why don't you want to believe me?' he demanded harshly.

'Do you recall the conversation we had that night you forced me to have dinner with you at your home? You scoffed at marriage, and afterwards you made it quite clear that you wanted me to become your . . . mistress.' She virtually choked on the word. 'I refused you, and the very next weekend you had Sylvia Summers staying with you.'

'I can——'

'Afterwards you had the gall to tell me that all I had to do was to say "yes" to you, and you'd send Sylvia packing,' she continued blindly as if he had not interrupted. 'What sort of an opinion am I supposed to have of a man who could make a callous remark like that about a woman he'd just spent a passionate few days with?'

'I never touched her.'

'Oh, *really*, Dane!' she protested cynically. 'Do you expect me to believe that?'

'I thought I could shake off what I felt for you, but I couldn't. You were there between us all the time, and . . . dammit, I couldn't touch her!'

There was something about him now, something in his eyes that made her heart beat a shade faster, and her limbs were trembling beneath her when he continued to speak.

'I told her it was over between us, but she wouldn't believe me, and when she arrived uninvited at my home this afternoon I told her the truth rather bluntly and brutally.'

'You told her you wanted me?' she asked, her words a mere whisper.

'I told her I wanted to marry you.' He smiled cynically at the look of surprise that flashed across her tired face. 'I decided it was only fair to be honest with her, and as a result she became determined to make it as difficult as hell for me to convince you of my sincerity.'

His hands were spanning her slim waist, their warmth

through the silk of her dress sending exciting little tremors racing along her receptive nerves, and she asked a little breathlessly, 'Why do you want to marry me?'

'You're an extremely cool, proficient young woman, Jessica, and right from the start you were a challenge to me. You're not only an excellent doctor, you're also a remarkably good pilot, and I had to find out if you were human too,' he smiled faintly. 'I mocked you for becoming emotionally involved with your patients, but somehow you taught me that there was more to doctoring than just the physical side of it; that there's a psychological angle to it as well. Most of all, I think, I admire your courage, and . . .' A muscle jerked in his jaw, and something resembling a remembered fear lurked in his eyes. 'My God, Jessica, I've never been so frightened in all my life as on that day when you climbed into that truck to help the injured man in the cab. I knew then that if that truck slipped over the edge, taking you with it, I would lose a vital part of my existence, and it was that thought that drove me nearly out of my mind.'

'Dane . . .' she breathed, loving the sweet agony of his hands as they tightened about her waist, and she swayed towards him even before he drew her closer to his hard, muscled body.

'I love you, Jessica,' he murmured the words she had thought she would never hear, and his voice was vibrant with emotion as he rubbed his rough cheek against hers and sought that frantic little pulse at the base of her throat with his lips. 'I love every damned silly little thing about you. The way you walk, and the way that husky note in your voice deepens when you're emotionally disturbed. I love the way your eyes crease at the corners when you laugh, and the way they flash fire when you're angry.' He raised his head suddenly, his eyes probing hers until it felt as if he were delving into the secret recesses of her soul. 'Take pity on me, Jessica. I've never been so desperate for the need of a woman's love and, confound it, never has my entire existence depended on it.'

She was shaking so much now with the wonder of it all, that she couldn't speak, but the secrets of her heart were laid bare in her eyes, and he groaned, almost as if he were afraid to believe what he saw there.

'For pity's sake, Jessica, don't torment me like this!'

'I love you,' she managed somehow, her hands straying across his broad chest to become entwined behind his strong neck. 'Haven't I made it embarrassingly obvious to you on so many occasions?'

'How could I be sure when you never said anything,' he accused, but desire leapt like a flame in his eyes as they roamed every inch of her face before lingering on her soft, quivering mouth.

'You never said anything either,' she protested weakly.

'I did tell you that I wanted you.'

'That wasn't very encouraging for a girl who'd always lived according to certain principles, and where you're concerned, Dane, I became terribly greedy,' she confessed unsteadily. 'I wanted much, much more than that from you.'

'I think you're going to get more than you ever bargained for,' he issued a warning against her lips, and then she was swept up into the vortex of his passion, matching his hunger with a hunger of her own.

His hands caressed her a little wildly, moulding her to him until she felt his need as strongly as she felt her own, but she was aware, too, of a certain restraint in his love-making, and she loved him all the more for it.

'That night in Venda, after the snake dance ceremony,' Dane began at length, urging her towards the sofa and drawing her down beside him, 'I hadn't planned to make love to you, but——'

'I know,' she interrupted, tracing the strong line of his jaw with tender, loving fingers. 'It was a mad, magical

night, and I—I wouldn't have felt so ashamed of the part
I played in it if I'd known then that you loved me as
much as I loved you, but instead I thought . . .'

'You thought I was merely trying to satisfy my lustful
desires,' he finished for her with a faintly mocking smile,
and when she buried her hot face against his shoulder his
arms tightened about her. 'If Sister Ravele hadn't interrupted us you would have discovered exactly how much I
loved you.' His lips against her ear sent little shivers of
pleasure racing through her. 'You were going to let me
make love to you that night, weren't you?'

'Yes,' she confessed unashamedly. 'I—I couldn't somehow help myself, but I'm not making excuses for the way
I behaved. I wanted you; it was as plain and simple as
that.'

His lips found hers and all her longing and despair was
in that kiss, but when desire flared between them she drew
away from him slightly, and turned her face into his
shoulder once more.

'Do you think your parents would object if I made
arrangements for us to be married next Saturday?' Dane
asked eventually, and she was too tired and happy to be
surprised by his haste as she wrapped her arms about his
waist and nestled closer.

'I don't think they'll have any objection, but what
about my contract with Peter?'

'I shan't mind if you continue working until your contract has expired,' Dane replied, rubbing his cheek against
hers and drawing her closer into the circle of his arms.

'And after that?' she asked tentatively, a smile curving
her lips.

'We'll let time take care of itself.' He raised his head
slightly, and there was a surprising warmth and tenderness
in his eyes which seemed to melt her bones, but that look
was replaced swiftly by a devilish gleam. 'Do you think
your father will be satisfied with the cattle Chief Cedric

insisted I should use for the purchase of a wife?'

'Don't be ridiculous!' she laughed, then she tilted her head and glanced up at him curiously. 'What have you done with them, if I may know?'

'I gave them to the faithful Jonas who has looked after me for so many years, and I told him to get himself a good wife who could keep the house in order, and take care of the children—if at that time you still have a yen for doctoring.'

'Oh, Dane,' Jessica murmured unsteadily, burying her hot face against his shoulder, but he prised it out again so that he could look down into her dark, luminous eyes.

'You're blushing,' he grinned.

'I know,' she smiled tremulously. 'You have that shattering and embarrassing effect on me.'

'Do I?'

His lips trailed a sensually destructive path from her ear to the base of her throat, then back again to move on to her eager, waiting lips, but by this time her heart was beating so hard and fast that she was reminded of the primitive, rhythmic beating of the drums on that night they had been privileged to watch the dance of the snake. That primitive beat was vibrating through her again, stirring her emotions to a wild crescendo as Dane altered their position until she was lying full length on the sofa with his lean, hard body imprisoning her, and his fingers were impatient as they pulled down the zip of her dress and undid the catch of her bra. Her breasts swelled in response to the light, sensually arousing caress of his hands, and she was like driftwood on the rising crest of that ecstatic wave of desire.

A tiny shred of sanity brought to mind Chief Cedric's parting words. 'A man is like a python when he is ready to seek his mate. His hunger is swift and strong when he uncoils, and when he strikes there is no escape.'

He could have been referring to Dane, for his hunger,

swift and strong, lashed her like a storm, and in her tired but happy state, she was more vulnerable than she had ever been before.

'Dane!' she gasped, her blood flowing like liquid fire through her veins. 'Darling, please . . .'

Desire still smouldered in the eyes that looked down into hers when he raised himself up on one elbow. 'You want me to wait?'

'Would it be asking too much?' she pleaded softly, her dark eyes a little anxious as she slid her hands tenderly over his sleek, dark head until her fingers came to rest in the nape of his neck. 'Dane, would it?'

There was no doubting the love that she saw burning in his eyes, nor the tenderness in the smile that curved his often harsh mouth.

'You're worth waiting for, my Jessica,' he said and, getting to his feet, he drew her up with him. 'It's time you went to bed. It's nearly two o'clock, and I'm certainly not going to start our life together by taking advantage of a girl who's almost asleep on her feet.'

His fingers traced the lines of weariness beneath her eyes, then he kissed her lingeringly on her soft mouth.

'I'll see you tomorrow,' he said, picking up his jacket, and he blew her a kiss from the door before he closed it quietly behind him.

'I'll see you tomorrow,' his words echoed happily through her mind when she eventually crawled into bed. There was still so much to talk about, but it could wait until tomorrow, and she promptly went to sleep with a smile of tender, joyous happiness curving her lips.

Harlequin Plus

A WORD ABOUT THE AUTHOR

Yvonne Whittal's childhood was spent in Port Elizabeth, on the southern tip of Africa. She recalls dreaming of the day she would be able to travel to unknown countries.

At a very early age she began scribbling stories. Her ambition to be a writer resurfaced after her marriage and the birth of three daughters. She enrolled in a writing course, began submitting short stories to publishers and, with each rejection letter, became all the more determined.

Turning to the task of writing a full-length book, Yvonne was encouraged by a young woman with whom she was working—an avid reader of romance fiction and a helpful critic.

For Yvonne Whittal, there is no greater satisfaction than writing. "The characters become part of my life," she says, "and when I come to the end of each novel, realizing that I now have to part with manuscript, it is like saying farewell to dear and trusted friends."

Legacy of
PASSION

BY CATHERINE KAY

A love story begun long ago comes full circle...

Venice, 1819: Contessa Allegra di Rienzi, young, innocent, unhappily married. She gave her love to Lord Byron—scandalous, irresistible English poet. Their brief, tempestuous affair left her with a shattered heart, a few poignant mementos—and a daughter he never knew about.

Boston, today: Allegra Brent, modern, independent, restless. She learned the secret of her great-great-great-grandmother and journeyed to Venice to find the di Rienzi heirs. There she met the handsome, cynical, blood-stirring Conte Renaldo di Rienzi, and like her ancestor before her, recklessly, hopelessly lost her heart.

Now's your chance to discover the earlier
books in this exciting series.

Choose from this list of great
SUPERROMANCES!

#8 BELOVED INTRUDER   Jocelyn Griffin

#9 SWEET DAWN OF DESIRE   Meg Hudson

#10 HEART'S FURY   Lucy Lee

#11 LOVE WILD AND FREE   Jocelyn Haley

#12 A TASTE OF EDEN   Abra Taylor

#13 CAPTIVE OF DESIRE   Alexandra Sellers

#14 TREASURE OF THE HEART   Pat Louis

#15 CHERISHED DESTINY   Jo Manning

#16 THIS DARK ENCHANTMENT   Rosalind Carson

#17 CONTRACT FOR MARRIAGE   Megan Alexander

#18 DANCE OF DESIRE   Lisa Lenore

#19 GIVE US FOREVER   Constance F. Peale

#20 JOURNEY INTO LOVE   Jessica Logan

#21 RIVER OF DESIRE   Abra Taylor

#22 MIDNIGHT MAGIC   Christine Hella Cott

#23 FROM THIS BELOVED HOUR   Willa Lambert

#24 CALL OF THE HEART   Wanda Dellamere

#25 INFIDEL OF LOVE   Casey Douglas

SUPERROMANCE

Complete and mail this coupon today!

- -

Worldwide Reader Service

In the U.S.A.
1440 South Priest Drive
Tempe, AZ 85281

In Canada
649 Ontario Street
Stratford, Ontario N5A 6W2

Please send me the following SUPERROMANCES. I am enclosing my check or money order for $2.50 for each copy ordered, plus 75¢ to cover postage and handling.

☐ # 8	☐ # 14	☐ # 20
☐ # 9	☐ # 15	☐ # 21
☐ # 10	☐ # 16	☐ # 22
☐ # 11	☐ # 17	☐ # 23
☐ # 12	☐ # 18	☐ # 24
☐ # 13	☐ # 19	☐ # 25

Number of copies checked @ $2.50 each = $_____
N.Y. and Ariz. residents add appropriate sales tax $_____
Postage and handling $_____.75

TOTAL $_____

I enclose_____
(Please send check or money order. We cannot be responsible for cash sent through the mail.)
Prices subject to change without notice.

NAME_____
(Please Print)

ADDRESS_____APT. NO._____

CITY_____

STATE/PROV._____

ZIP/POSTAL CODE_____

Offer expires February 28, 1983   21156000000